Enoch Fitch Burr

Sunday Afternoons

A Book for Little People

Enoch Fitch Burr

Sunday Afternoons
A Book for Little People

ISBN/EAN: 9783744746366

Printed in Europe, USA, Canada, Australia, Japan

Cover: Foto ©Andreas Hilbeck / pixelio.de

More available books at **www.hansebooks.com**

SUNDAY AFTERNOONS.

A BOOK FOR LITTLE PEOPLE.

By E. F. BURR, D. D.,

AUTHOR OF "ECCE CŒLUM," ETC.

New York:

NELSON & PHILLIPS.

CINCINNATI: HITCHCOCK & WALDEN.

SUNDAY-SCHOOL DEPARTMENT.

CONTENTS.

SUNDAY AFTERNOONS.

I.

THE SOUL.

IF I should ask you to tell me the names of all the things you have ever seen, you would think it very strange, and perhaps would say, " Why, sir, I could not *begin* to do such a thing. There are houses, flowers, trees, cattle, birds, men, lightning, fires, clouds, rivers, hills, fruit, grain, sun, moon, stars—and ten thousand things besides. Why, sir, I could not *begin* to tell all the things I have seen, they are so many."

You are right. Neither you nor the greatest man can tell even all the wonderful things, above, beneath, around you, that can be seen in a single day. How beautiful many of these things are! Did you never take up a little flower, or a little shell, or a little butterfly, and hold it close to your eyes and see what soft, rich colors, and what bright, wavy, graceful lines there were all about it? How grand many of these things are—the great hills with their tops in the clouds; the great rivers, bearing up the heavy vessels as if they were so many feathers, and sweeping them off into the broad sea; the great world itself, which, as you have been told at school, is thousands of miles around and holds hundreds of millions of people; above all, the glorious sun in the sky, a million of times larger than this world, and so bright that the strongest eyes dare not look it full in the face! How awful are some of the things you now and then see—for just think of the lightning as it shoots its forked tongue toward you; the storm that, black as night, comes down on the woods, and makes them toss and break in the roaring wind! And then what wise and beautiful contrivances there are in almost every thing you see—in the bird that darts so swiftly through the air; in the fish that cuts the water so easily; in the squirrel that runs so nimbly from stone to stone and from branch to branch; in your own bodies, with hands to catch, and feet to run, and eyes to see, and ears to hear, and tongue to talk, and a hundred other things to do as many other things with !

Now I want you to attend well to what I am about to say to you. I am about to say a very important thing, one which many older persons than you need to hear. It is this. These things which you see are not the *only* real things; nor are they even the most beautiful, grand, important, and nicely made of real things. I know of something that is greatly better in all these respects. People sometimes call it *spirit.* No eyes such as we have ever saw it: no such eyes ever can see it. It is every-where about you, and yet, however sharp you may look, you will never be able to catch the first glimpse of it. Your eyes are bright and young; whatever eyes can do no doubt they can do; but this I know, that they never yet saw that wonderful thing called *spirit*, and never will see it. You can see what it *does* very often—you can hear and feel what it does almost every moment; but, as to the thing itself, you cannot ever set eyes or hands on it. And yet it is a *real* thing—as real as any rock or tree—a very beautiful, and grand, and important thing, too, and full of marks of glorious wisdom—much more so than such things as flowers, mountains, storms, suns. You cannot think how great and important a thing this same spirit is, and how important it is that you should know about it, though you cannot see it. It is because it is so important that I will now try to tell you something about it as well as I can.

There are different sorts of spirit, just as there are different sorts among the things that you see. There is the black iron, the white silver, and the yellow gold; there is the common stone of the field and street, the white, smooth marble which you see in the church-yard, and the dazzling diamond set in the crown of a king; there is the dull clod that the plow turns over, the flesh of your cheek, soft and red with youth, and the quick, bright lightning that plays and darts so fiercely about the edge of the thunder-cloud : these all are things that can be seen, only different sorts of them. Just so there are very different sorts of spirit, and especially three sorts which we happen to know very well. One is called *soul*, another is called *angel*, and still another is called *God*. I will not speak to you about all of these just now : only about the first, the *soul*. You have heard this word before many a time ; but not so many, I dare say, that you cannot hear it many more times without hearing it too much.

Somewhere within your body—I will not undertake to say where—is a something which you cannot see any more than if it were at the other side of the world; which has no weight, nor color, nor size, nor shape that we know of, but which is very, very active, and can think and feel and choose. This is what looks out at your eyes, and pictures itself in your whole face, and speaks in the words you use. This is what sets your hands and feet in motion, makes you able to play or work or study, makes you able to see and hear and smell and taste. Without the soul within you, you would be like a dead person— stiff, silent, doing nothing, knowing nothing. When you look at a watch you see the hands moving over its white face, and the faint tick never fails to reach your ears at every second; but what makes the watch go and beat the time is not any thing that you see; it is something inside that keeps silently pulling on the wheels; it is the spring all covered up out of sight. And what puts all the motion and sound into that body of yours is not any thing that you see, but that unseen thing within which thinks, feels, and chooses, and which men call the *soul*.

I say that you do not see your soul. No wonder, for it is within you. But you might even take a human body all to pieces, and watch very carefully while doing it, and yet you would not find the soul anywhere. Your eyes are not sharp enough to see such things, just as they are not sharp enough to see the air in this room and a great many things besides. No, you can neither see nor handle the soul; but still we can know perfectly well that every body has a soul living in it just as a man does in a house. Suppose you should stand before a house and see smoke coming out of the chimney; see windows and doors and blinds open and shut; see curtains let down and raised; see lights shining through the windows; and moving about from room to room, and sometimes making shadows, as of persons, across the panes; hear music coming from it in many well-known tunes—you would have no

doubt somebody lived in the house, though
you never happened to see any one plainly
showing himself at the window or coming
out at the door. Even if you should find
the door locked, and, on breaking it open,
should find nobody in any of the rooms,
you would still be sure that somebody has
been living there and has either hid or
slipped out at the back door while you
were getting in—especially if you should
find all sorts of furniture about, and even
fires burning, table set, food all ready to
be eaten, and should hear sounds as of
feet going away. You would say, "Sure
enough some one has been living here, but
for some reason does not wish to be seen."
So we know by a thousand signs that
something lives in our bodies, very different from them, that thinks, feels, chooses,
remembers, hopes, fears, loves, hates, en-
joys, suffers, is bad or good. It speaks in
the face, shines in the eyes, talks with the
tongue, works with the hands, walks with
the feet, does right or wrong with the

whole body: and when learned people look into the body they find it all fitted up as splendidly for a soul to live in as ever a palace was for a king.

Now there are some things that I wish to tell you about this soul that lives in the body just as if it were a house. We do not know all about it although it is so near us, and we carry it about with us all the while. For example, we do not know what it is made of, what shape it has, how it moves the hands and feet and other parts of the body, how it sees with the eyes and hears with the ears, how it is fastened to the body, or exactly in what part of the body it lives. A great many such things we do not know. But many other things we do know, and I will now tell you some of them.

Souls are *very many*—as many at least as there are living human bodies in the world. Each of us has a soul in his body. Every little child, however small and wherever living, has a soul, as well as every grown-up person. All the black people, such as live in Africa; all the red people, such as once lived here and were called Indians; all the olive people, such as live in some parts of Asia; these all have souls as well as white people. So have all poor and homely and ignorant and bad persons, as well as the rich and fair and wise and good—all the poor heathen away at the ends of the earth, worshiping idols, as well as such people as live here and fill our churches on Sundays. Do not forget this; for some persons act as if they thought that only a few have souls—a few rich or great or wise people. And most men seem to forget for a large part of the time that they themselves and their children, to say nothing about the heathen, have souls to be taken care of. You yourself are in danger of living just as if you have no soul. So I charge you to remember that there is a soul within every human body.

These souls are not all exactly alike.

Very far from it. They differ as much from each other as do the bodies in which they live. One is large, another small. One is strong, another weak. One is swift, another slow. Some are bright and strong and swift for some things, others for other things. One seems made to fill great places and do great things, another seems made for a small place and work. Indeed, souls differ as much as do houses and trees; and you know that scarcely any two of these are exactly alike. We could not bring all our souls to be exactly alike if we should try. Some seem to try, but they never succeed. And it is not best that they should. We need to have souls differ from each other so that they may fill different places and do different sorts of work. So they are made very unlike as to what they are able to do, and as to what they like to do. Every teacher or father has to remember this very often. And now you understand a part of the reason why ministers and Sunday-school teachers try to talk to children and others in so many different ways. It is because souls differ as much among themselves as do the leaves on the trees when the first frosts have touched them. What different colors, as well as shapes and sizes and ways of hanging! No two are alike.

All souls began only a little while ago. If I should ask you how old you are, you would answer, six, ten, fifteen years, as the case may be. This tells how old your body is, and it also tells how old your soul is. It is a new thing. A very short time ago nobody knew any thing about it—it did not know any thing about itself. There was no thinking, no feeling, no choosing, no any thing that belongs to it now. But on a sudden it began to be. Almost as it were yesterday, your soul awoke in its fresh, new body—remembering nothing, and looking out through the windows of your new eyes on a world that seemed quite new and strange. It felt itself just beginning to live. And it was.

Some souls in the world are older than yours, but none of them go back very far. A hundred years ago scarcely a single one of them was to be found. I am speaking now of souls that are living at the present time in the millions of human bodies all over the world. And, for my part, I do not believe that there is a human soul *anywhere* that is much more than six thousand years old. Perhaps this seems a long time to you, but it does not to me. At any rate, you will agree with me that it is but a very short time since *your* soul began.

When souls begin to be, every thing about them is very weak and small. You know how weak the body of the little babe is. It cannot walk ; it cannot hold itself up ; it cannot even creep at the very first. Some one must do every thing for it, it is so helpless. If left to itself it would die. Now the soul of this babe is just as weak as its body. It knows scarcely any thing, it can do scarcely any thing. And when the babe becomes the little child that runs about, its knowledge and strength of all sorts, though greater, are still small. They grow somewhat as the little body grows; but every child is far from having as large and strong a soul as a full-grown man. So the laws put him under the care of parents and others, who are to teach him, and show him what he must do, and bring him up. God also does the same. And, instead of being headstrong and wise in their own conceit, he bids them be modest, respectful, teachable, and obedient—as becomes mere beginners in life. I have known some children who seemed to think themselves as wise as Solomon, and who scorned to be taught and governed by anybody. And they were very unlovely and very foolish. I hope you will not be like them. On the contrary, always remember that all young souls are small and weak.

Souls not only begin very small and weak, but, what is a great deal worse, they

begin *very sinful.* You know all too
well what it is to be sinful—what it is to
do wrong, and what it is to find it easier
and pleasanter to do wrong than to do
right. You have *tried* it. And all have
tried it from the time they were born.
Among all the millions of souls that have
lived, there have been only three that began good, and only one soul that both began and continued good. I think you do
not need to have me tell you who these
were. All the rest have been bad at the
beginning, and more or less bad all their
days. And, to-day, there is not a single
soul in all the world but is sinful and
always has been. The best children have
evil hearts. You do a great many wrong
things, and always have done them; and
it is because your soul is out of order, in-
clined to do evil rather than good; as we
say, *corrupt.* I will not now try to tell
you how this happened. It is enough for
the present for you to know that it *did*
happen, and that nothing worse could pos-

sibly have befallen us. There is no trouble like a bad heart. It is much worse than a sickly body. People are sometimes born with this, and we are sorry for them. But a sickly, corrupt, sinful soul—a soul that is all the while trying to be wrong and do wrong, as water tries to run down hill—is much worse. All our other troubles come from this. If there had never been any sin there would never have been any sorrow. All the pains and groans and tears we know of came from this root. I hope you will remember this also, and always think it a very sad thing to have a sinful soul. And it would be a much sadder thing than it is if one could never get rid of this sinfulness; but this every one can do—by degrees. By degrees he can get the better of this soul-sickness, just as we sometimes get the better of a sickness of the body. We call a doctor, we take some medicine, we get a good nurse, and after a while we begin to mend. We have less and less pain, our eyes grow brighter, the color comes back to our cheeks, our appetite comes slowly back, we get new strength day by day, at last we walk abroad and go about our business as usual. We are well.

So we can get the better of our sins, and indeed of almost every thing about the soul that we do not like. I have told you how weak and narrow the soul is at first. But souls are *growing* things. They can be made to grow without stopping as long as we live. Your body must stop growing after a little while, but your soul can grow and grow and still grow without end. It will never get so large and strong that it cannot be larger and stronger. It can always be wiser and better and more powerful to-day than it was yesterday. I do not say that it *will* certainly improve in this way, only that it *can* do so. There is nothing that need hinder. If it should live forever it could grow forever. The trees grow about so tall and then stop: they never grow any more, though they live a thousand years afterward. So with every sort of animals—each has a certain small size which it never goes beyond, however long it lives. Nothing can keep such things growing. No care, no food, no rest, no nursing. They will even become smaller and weaker as they become old; but the soul—every soul, your soul—can be so managed that every year it lives shall see it brighter and fairer and stronger and larger. It is more elastic than any thing we know of. It is like a certain tent which we read about in the fables. It could always be stretched a little more. To-day it covers but a single man. By and by it will cover his whole family. When that family has grown into a tribe the tent will still be found capacious enough to cover them all. And when the tribe has become a nation and fills all Arabia with its people, all its millions will be sheltered just as well by that ever-growing silk as was the first man who used it.

Now I come to something that makes this fact very important. This is that souls will have an opportunity to grow and improve *forever*. They have but a short life to look backward to, but they have a very long life to look forward to. Just think of it—this young soul of yours is to live FOREVER, FOREVER! It has no death about it. You could not kill it if you would; nor could the strongest man that ever breathed. Sickness cannot touch it. It cannot be pierced, or crushed, or burned, or drowned. Battles and armies even, with their sharp swords and shotted cannon, cannot make an end of it or even hurt it. Hundreds after hundreds of years will pass, thousands after thousands, millions after millions, and yet not one wonderful soul of all the many now on the earth will have ceased to be, or even have grown old. They will be as fresh as ever; nay, fresher and stronger and more active as the ages go by! Is it not a great thing to think of that these souls of ours that so lately began will go on living, acting, thinking, feeling, growing without end?

But though all our souls will live for-ever, none of them will live always, or even a great while, in the bodies we now have. Sometimes a man's house is burned and then he moves into another. Always it grows old and crazy, and at last falls down, and then the man is found living in another. So it will be with the body-houses which our souls live in. Some of them will go to pieces before their time— burned up by fevers, torn down by what people call accidents—perhaps before an-other year has gone. Others will last several years, growing larger, stronger, and firmer at first, and then weaker and weaker, till at last they will become so old and tottering that our souls can stay in them no longer. The same day and hour that they fall the souls will go out to find somewhere else to live.

Where will they go? Go somewhere they *must*, for they must live and live forever, and they can no longer live in their old homes. Where will they go? Now it so happens that I can answer this question just as well as if I had already seen souls go out of their bodies and had followed them. I have been told by One who knows—One that it were wicked and dreadful not to believe—that they will go to one of two places. One of these places is that " Happy Land " of which you have so often sung. It is a most beautiful place. You never dreamed of any thing half so beautiful. Your parents and others that love you could not wish any thing better for you than that you might go at last to live in such a place. A man once had a chance to look at it, and it seemed to him as though it were all covered with gold and precious stones, while waters clear as crystal sparkled, and green fields smiled, and glorious trees waved leaf and fruit over beautiful people with crowns on their heads and dresses white as snow, and the strangest, sweetest music fell upon his ear.

You cannot think how happy and how good the souls are that get to this wonderful place. They never do any thing wrong. They know nothing about trouble. To live is a wonderful joy : they could not be happier. This is one place to which our souls may go when they leave the bodies in which they now live. Then there is another place, just as unlike this as unlike can be. Instead of being the brightest and loveliest place that ever was, it is the darkest and most frightful. Instead of being the happiest and holiest, it is the most wretched and wicked. There is nothing like it for badness among all bad places. It almost makes me faint to speak about it, and even to think about it. You could not wish anybody any thing worse than that he might live forever in such a place. O, it is so horrible and wicked !

To one or the other of these places all our souls must go when they leave their bodies. But very likely this answer will not satisfy you. It ought not to satisfy you. Of course you want to know to which of these two places—the one so glorious and the other so dreadful—*your* soul will have to go when you die. Well, I can answer this question too, and you can make sure it will be a right answer, for I had it from One who knows all about such things, and who would not deceive me on any account. You ask me to which of those two places, the one so bright and the other so bad, your soul will go when the breath leaves your body. I answer, that depends on how you behave while the soul is still in your body. Remember that *all depends on how you behave while the soul is still in your body.* If you behave in a certain way, your spirit will surely go to the beautiful land and stay there forever. It is what you are doing now that will settle where your soul will go. If you will be sorry for the wrong things you have done, and will pray Jesus, the Christian's Saviour, to forgive you, and will sincerely set yourself to love and serve him as long as you live, nothing more will be needed. Your precious soul will go up straight as a ray of light to Paradise (for that is one of the names of the happy country) the moment you breathe your last. But if you do not choose to do this, and die without having done it— whether that be to-morrow or fifty years hence—the consequence will be that your precious soul will go down straight to that dark country of which I have told you, never more to come back. So I have answered your question.

I said to you that spirit was a far more wonderful and important thing than any thing you can see, look where you will. You see that this is true even of souls— true of *your* soul. There is nothing that you have ever seen, or that others ever saw, half so grand, so wonderful, so precious, as is that unseen, thinking something that hides within your young body. It is that which does all your planning, feeling and choosing for you. It is that which knows and remembers; which loves and hates, fears and hopes; which does right and wrong, and can do either to almost any extent; which feels happiness and misery, and can feel either to almost any extent; which, though it has only just begun to be, will be forever either in a happy or wretched place, according as it shall choose to act in this world. Said I not truly that among things that your eyes can see there is nothing that for a moment can be thought worth so much as this? Now you see why it is that ministers preach and urge so Sabbath after Sabbath: it is because the people have souls, precious, undying, sinful, endangered souls. Now you see why missionaries are sent to distant countries: it is because the heathen living there have souls—precious, undying, sinful, endangered souls. Now you see why Sunday-schools are held, and so many good books and papers made for children. It is because they all have souls—precious, undying, endangered souls.

Now you see why it is that your good parents and other friends are at times so concerned about you, and pray for you so earnestly. It is because you have a soul within you—a precious, undying, endangered soul. Now you see why it is that I am writing this to you. Surely I should not have thought of writing to you at all, much less of writing to you about spirits and souls, had I not known that in every child lives a soul—precious, wonderful, endless, and in danger of being endlessly miserable and sinful, one which you need to think of, and value, and care for more than any thing else.

And now what I want of you is, that you take care of this soul of yours that is worth so much. If you do not take care of it, there is no use in your taking care of any thing else. Suppose a house is on fire. It is getting very hot, and all about the doors and the windows and the roof the flames are bursting out. You wonder why the little boy that you know to be in the house does not come out. You see him running by the windows every now and then. Why does he not come out? Suppose now you should find out that he was looking for pins, and bits of ribbon, and other such little things—trying to make sure of as many of them as he could —what would you think of him? You would say he was a very foolish boy, would you not? What good will his pins and ribbons do him if he burns up? Let him come out—let him save himself—and when he is far from danger he can go hunting his little things wherever he pleases. So I say to you, before all things save your souls. This is the thing to be done before play, before work, before study, before every thing. If you should never get to that "Happy Land" little good would any thing do you. But I hope you will try to get to it. And if you try, and try, and go on trying, you will succeed. It is not so hard a thing for those of your age to be sorry for their sins and learn to

love and please Christ as it is for those
who are older. Will you not do it? This
will save that soul of yours that is so
precious. This will make it happy forever
in that beautiful country to which it will
go as soon as your body dies. There are
many bright and beautiful children there.
No words can tell how they shine and
sing, with crowns on their heads and harps
in their hands! I hope to see them some
day; and I hope also to see you among
them, as bright and fair and happy as any.
What a pity if you should miss such a
glorious place—you whom the Saviour
meant when he said so kindly, " Suffer little
children to come unto me, and forbid them
not: for of such is the kingdom of God."

There was once a great king who had
many beautiful jewels and robes and
crowns and scepters, and he thought that
they should not always lie in a dark room
and be seen by scarcely anybody; so he
had them all brought into the center of a
great building and placed on tables right

under a great window in the roof, so that
all his people and people from other lands
might come and see them. I went with
many others, and I saw well all those beautiful and costly things. But I noticed
that the king was very careful of his treasures. He plainly did not mean that any
of them should be stolen or harmed.
There was a strong iron railing about
them. There were soldiers to watch and
keep off the crowd. We could not touch
any thing. We could only·see the splendid show. That was all right. I did not
blame the king. He did as he should
have done. It was proper that his care
of his treasures should be as great as their
great value. See how you should do! A
soul is a far richer and fairer and more
costly treasure than ever shone in the
robes and thrones and diadems of kings.
You should take great care of it. You
should fence it off from harm as with soldiers and with rails of iron, for if you should
lose it the loss could never be made good.

II.

THE ANGELS.

THERE are things about you besides
what you can see—things just as real
as trees and hills and stars. I mean
spirits. These wonderful beings do all the
thinking and wishing and willing, all the
knowing and feeling, all the loving and
hating, all the hoping and fearing, all the
right-doing and wrong-doing, that is done
any where—and yet you never saw them,
and never can see them with such eyes as
you now have.

We know of at least three sorts of spirits—souls, angels, and God. When I last
met you I spent the time in telling about
souls—those beings which, hidden in our
bodies, do all our thinking and wishing
and willing. I will now tell you about
another kind of spirits, namely, *angels*.

A long time ago some soldiers were standing before a cave. They had been standing there all night to keep the dead person who had been laid in it from being carried away. Just as morning was coming—it was Sunday morning that was just beginning to touch the hills in the east—they suddenly heard a great noise and the ground shook under their feet, and they saw something like a man come down from the sky close to them, with a face bright as lightning and dress white as snow. They were so frightened, soldiers as they were, that they fainted away. But some good women who came along had better courage, and, though they did not dare to speak to so bright a being, they heard what he said to them. He told them what they came to the place for; that the dead body they expected to find was alive again and gone, and that if his friends would go to a certain mountain they should see him. This was an *angel*, or, rather, it was the body which an angel had put on. As nobody has ever seen a soul, only the body in which it lives, so nobody has ever seen angels, only the bodies which they have worn. But, for all that, we know a good deal about them, and you should understand that they are as much grander and brighter than our souls as that lightning-body which the soldiers saw was grander and brighter than such bodies as we have.

The angels are much more knowing than we are. They are a great deal wiser and stronger. I do not suppose that a whole army of men would be able to stand against one of them. Indeed, I happen to know that one night a single angel killed near two hundred thousand men; and it was done so quietly and easily that those sleeping by the side of the slain knew nothing of it till the morning came. Then they awoke and found the camp filled with dead. The angels are not obliged to creep along the ground as we do. They can fly through the sky swifter than any bird, swifter than any cannon-ball, swifter even than the swift lightning. We cannot get away from the earth if we try; the most we can do is to travel a little on it, and now and then go up a few hundred feet in a balloon. But the angels can fly away to the sun and stars, and can pass from star to star almost as quickly as you can think of its being done. If you want to go into a room you have to open a door or window; if you want to go to the other side of a hill you have to go over or around it; but an angel can pass right through walls of wood or stone just as if they were so much air.

Did you never read how it happened once in the olden time? Some friends of Jesus were together in a room, and the doors and windows were all shut and fastened for fear of the Jews. All at once Jesus stood in the midst of them. How did he get in? No door had opened, nor window. Could you have looked at the bolts and bars you would have found them quite untouched. Yet there he was. This shows you how easily angels may go any-where among us, and that not even the thickest prison walls can shut in or out these wonderful spirits.

The angels are very old. Long ago, when the world was young, men them-selves lived almost a thousand years—trees are now standing which must have stood more than three times that great time—and O how long, long a time that does seem to you, stretching out and out as if it would *never* end! But I have no idea this is any thing like as long as the angels have lived. I cannot say exactly how old they are, but I think that the youngest of them is older than the world—counting from the time when men began to live on it. Six thousand years, at least, have the angels lived—it may be six hundred thou-sand—and, what is even more wonderful, they show no sign of being old at all. They are just as fresh and strong as they ever were. They were never so wise, so

active, so mighty as they are at this moment. They are actually getting stronger
and stronger every day, instead of weaker
and weaker. " Is this so ? " you say ;
" then very likely they will never die.
This growing stronger for six thousand
years and more does not look like dying."
You are right. The angels will live *always*
—life-time after life-time, century after century, world-life after world-life, I had
almost said eternity after eternity.

Are they very many, these angels ? O
yes, wonderfully many ! There is no
counting them, they are so many. Not
long ago we were every day hearing of
our great armies at Washington and else-
where, all ready to fight for and against
their country. Could you have seen them
you would have said, " What a *sight* of
people ! " And then almost every country
in Europe has armies nearly as large as
we once had. But put theirs and ours together and they would not equal the
mighty armies of the angels. Sure I am

they are many times more than all the
people of the world. They are like the
leaves on the trees or the sands on the
sea-shore. Did you never hear of a little
boy whom his father took one day to the
beach to gather the yellow shells and play
in the soft white sand—and how the child
took up a handful of the sand and tried
to count all the little grains—and how
he soon became quite discouraged and
gave up the counting, and said, "Father,
there is *no end* of them!" Suppose he
had tried to count all the sands on all the
sea-shores of the world! As well might
one try to count the angels.

There are two sorts of angels, living in
two very different places. One sort are
perfectly good beings, and these live in
Heaven, that beautiful place to which
good men go when they die. The other
sort are very bad beings, and these live in
Hell, that dreadful place to which bad men
go at last. Once there was only one kind
of angels. They were all good and all

lived in Heaven. But a great many of them in some way became wicked, and after that they were cast out of their glorious home and were obliged to go and live in a place as bad as themselves. And that is *very* bad. Neither bad nor good angels are bad or good like men. The good are perfectly good and the bad are well-nigh perfectly bad—the one sort white as the whitest snow, the others black as ink. And so the place where the good angels live is the brightest and most beautiful that ever was known, and the place where the others live is the dreariest and worst—nothing like it anywhere. But you must not think that the angels stay in these places all the while. These places are only their homes. They go and come, just as men do. A man leaves his house and is gone all day—perhaps a good many days—and yet people call it his home, and say that is where he lives. Perhaps he goes a great distance—say to New York or Washington—perhaps he travels about on the other side of the ocean for a whole year, and yet people say this is his home, this is where he lives. In the same way we say that Heaven is the home of the good angels, and Hell the home of the bad, though none of them stay in these homes all the while, but, on the contrary, fly about and go away to very distant places, and stay away for a long time. I have no doubt that both kinds of them come as far as us, and make a long tarry too—especially the bad angels, because our world is so much pleasanter than theirs; but still Heaven is the place to which the good angels belong, and Hell is the place to which belong the bad angels.

The angels are not all equally great and strong and wise and high. It is with them as it is with men. Some men are strong, and some are very weak. Some know much, and some very little. Some are beautiful, and some are very homely. Some are private soldiers, some captains, some generals, and some kings and empe-

rors. They differ among themselves as
much as do the lakes and the mountains.
We have three small lakes in our own
small town, but these would be almost
nothing by the side of some of our great
western lakes stretching through hundreds
of miles. We have our large hills, and
any day you can see Mount Archer looking down pleasantly on them, as a father
does on his children ; but what would the
highest of these be by the side of the
Rocky Mountains and the Alps, their heads
white with everlasting snows? There is
just as much difference among the angels
in greatness and glory as there is among
mountains or lakes or men. Michael is a
leader and prince among the good angels,
Satan is the leader and prince among the
bad angels. And there was a time, now
long ago, when these two great spirits,
each with an army of lesser spirits under
him, fought against each other on the
plains of Heaven. Satan was conquered,
and he and his fell from Heaven as some

of you have seen the shooting-stars fall in November—only much more thickly. The sky was all ablaze with them.

In this country people often *change* their homes. A man sells out. He gets together all that he cares about, and puts it on a cart or in a boat, and goes away into another place to live. Still, some persons spend their whole lives in one place. The houses they were born in are the houses they live and die in. In England, the country from which our fathers came, it is no uncommon thing to find families which have been living on the same lands and in the same dwellings time out of mind—fathers, grandfathers, great-grandfathers, and away back for hundreds of years. They have never moved. They are proud of it, and hope they will never have any other homes while the world stands. It is not very likely they will have their wish, this is such a changing world. But I can tell you of some beings who never, never change their homes. I

mean the angels. It is true that the bad
angels made a change some thousands of
years ago, (and a very dreadful change it
was,) but there will be no more changes.
They will never have any other home than
the dreary, dreadful one they have had
ever since. And the angels who kept
their goodness will never have any other
than the bright, glorious home they have
always had. No, from this time forward
none of these spirits will ever change their
home; and the reason is, that none of
them will ever change their character.
Bad men often become very good men—
bad children often become very good children. Your parents and teachers are hoping that those of you who have evil, wicked
hearts will one day come to have good
hearts instead of the bad. Such things
are happening every day, especially among
the children who go to the Sunday-school.
I have read of a boy so bad that he had
to be sent to prison. He would swear and
lie and steal, and when a kind man tried

to help him and teach him better things he had no gratitude, but tried to steal from that best friend. But that friend would not give up the poor wicked boy, and after awhile, though he was so wicked at first, he came to be good. People hardly knew him, the change was so great. It was like the change sometimes made in an old house. The carpenter repairs, takes away, adds, and at last you hardly know the building. It is as good as new. On some accounts it is better than a new house could be. Such was the change in that little boy. He was quite another child, much to the wonder of all who knew him. And all of you can be changed from bad to good in the same way. But such a thing will never happen to the bad angels. They will always stay bad, and the good angels will always stay good. A change there will be, but not of this kind. The good angels will get stronger and stronger in their goodness every day, while the bad angels will be getting worse and worse. And so it will be that none of them will ever change their home. If it is Heaven, there they will stay forever. If it is that other world, which it is so hard to name because it is so dreadful, there they will stay forever. Each in the place suited to his character.

But now, perhaps, some of you are thinking something like this, " What have *we* to do with these angels? What use in *our* hearing so much about them, if they do not live in this world ? " Let me tell you, by bringing back to your minds what I have already told you. The two worlds where these angels live are the places to which when we die all of us must go. We must have, by and by, one or the other sort of angels for company, and have them for company always. And there is another thing to be thought of. Though the homes of the angels are in the two distant worlds I have spoken of, yet these spirits are by no means shut up in them, but spend much of their time in

this world right among us. Good angels
and bad—they are flying about us all the
while. They are in the fields where men
are at work, in the stores where men buy
and sell, in the boats where men are fish-
ing, along the roads where men are walk-
ing and riding, in the houses where families sit together, even in the churches
where we come to learn and do holy
things. They are at our ears, our eyes,
our tongues, our hands, our hearts. They
put good and bad thoughts into our
minds; they try to get us to do this and
to do that; they help us and they hinder
us; they fight for us and they fight against
us. The holy angels try to do us all the
good they can—the wicked angels try to
do us all the hurt they can. The good
spirits want to have us good like themselves, and do all they can to make us so:
the bad spirits want to have us bad like
themselves, and do all they can to make us
so. And they do not forget the *children*,
down to the youngest. I suppose they

are just as busy at the ears and in the heart of a child of six years as of a man of sixty—the good pulling him upward, and the bad pulling him downward. None of them can make even the smallest child do as they please: all they can do is to tempt him, to persuade him. If he has a mind to refuse them he can do so, and can drive them quite away from him. All he has to do is to say NO to them, and to *keep* saying it, and they will leave him, whether they are good angels or evil ones. And if he wants to keep them let him say YES to them, and *keep* saying it, and they will stay by him without fail.

So you must never think yourselves alone. When your fathers and mothers and playmates are out of sight, and on looking about you every-where, above and below and around, not a sign of a person can be seen, then remember that there are many beings besides those which the eye can see. For aught you can know the air about you may be all alive with people—

people whom you cannot see, but who can see you and hear you and know all you are doing. It may be as if you were in a city when you seem most alone. Do not forget that the world is full of angels, bad and good, and that at no moment can you be sure that thousands of them are not watching every thing you do.

There was once a good man whom a certain king wished to take prisoner. So this king sent a great army to the city where the man was. And when his servant looked over the wall and saw so many waving banners and glittering spears he was much afraid. It seemed as if nothing could save him. Then his master asked God to open his eyes. . All at once, instead of finding himself all alone amid a host of enemies, he saw the sky about him filled with protecting angels. Of course he was not afraid any more. When he thought himself all alone there were thousands and thousands of angels about him. So it may be with you.

Besides, do not forget that there is a great struggle going on between the two kinds of angels as to which shall have you with them. The good angels want you, and the bad angels want you. The one want to have you wise and holy, and to take you up with them to the beautiful world where they most delightfully live; the others want to make you foolish and wicked, and to take you down with them to that wicked world where they are to live forever in shame and punishment. And so they are struggling and pulling you different ways. The reason you do not feel it is that the pulling is on your *hearts* and *wills*, and not on your bodies. They are trying to persuade you—trying about as hard as they can—to have you be their friends and go with them where they will always live. And you must think what you will do—must choose on which side you will be. On which side shall we find you?

Would you not rather have the good

angels for friends—those bright, beautiful
beings who love you so much ? To tell
the truth the bad angels do not love you
at all. They do not love anybody. All
they want is to deceive you, and hurt you,
and make you wretched forever. They
will be as glad as such wicked beings can
be to make you as wicked as themselves
and drag you down to that black world
where they belong, and there torment
you as badly as can be without end—
they hate you so much. But the good
angels love you as much as the bad ones
hate you. If they can only get you to be
on their side and to do as they do—to be
good like themselves, and go with them to
their golden homes in the sky—it will
make them very happy.

How your parents' faces will sometimes
shine upon you with love and joy when they
see you doing well, and feel encouraged to
think that you will grow up to be a comfort
and honor to them ! You would at such
times see much brighter faces than those of

father and mother shining joyfully upon
you, if you could then see the good angels
which are all about you. The sky is all
in a glory with their glad and thankful
looks—they love you so much.

Now which angels would you rather live
with always? What place would you rather
live in always—the brightest and fairest
and happiest world that ever was known,
or the blackest and wretchedest? I know
what you would say, " We want to go to
the Happy Land. Every one of us wants
to find his home at last with those bright
angels, brighter than summer or the stars,
and who are as loving as they are bright."

But, that you may do this, you must
begin now to *be like* the good angels.
While you are in this world you must
learn to be good like them—you must
learn to love right-doing and to hate
wrong-doing, just as they do. It is not
easy for you to do this. You have evil
hearts which help the bad spirits to lead
you in evil ways. But you can get the

better of them if you try hard.   There is
a great Spirit, far greater than they,
stronger and wiser than all of them together, who will help you against them if
you will ask Him.   There is a great Saviour who loves children and is mightier
than all the evil angels and your evil
hearts put together, and who will save
you from them if you will ask him.   I
hope to tell you more about these great
helpers soon; but you know something
about them already, and when you feel it
hard to be good you must not forget to
ask them to help you.   Ask them to take
away your evil hearts.   Ask them to take
your part against the bad angels and Satan their king.   In this way you will
drive those evil ones away from you, and
the bright, good angels will most gladly
take you for their own, and watch over
you day and night, and help you to be
better and better; and by and by, when
you die, they will gather about you in a
golden cloud and carry you up with joy-

ful songs to your home in heaven. And *such* a home! I have seen many places which I thought very beautiful. I have seen pictures of places which I thought more beautiful still, and I can shut my eyes and build up in my thoughts glorious palaces and cities and countries far richer and fairer than I ever saw in the finest paintings; but even these thought-pictures, when we have done our best to make them lovely, give but a very poor idea of that glorious land to which you and I may go if we will.

III.

GOD.

I SHALL speak to you next about the greatest Being ever known — about GOD. This is one of his names, the name we most hear; but he has many other names, such as Lord, Jehovah, Creator, Almighty.

I hope you will remember how I have come to speak to you of this great Being. I first told you of two sorts of things— the things that can be seen, and the things that cannot be seen with such eyes as we have. People sometimes call these two sorts of things matter and spirit. I did not say much to you about matter—about the trees, the flowers, the fields, the rivers, the mountains, the stars, although these are very curious and beautiful things—because they are not so beautiful and important as the other sort of things. So I went on to tell you about spirits. I said we knew at least three kinds of spirits—souls, angels, and God. Souls I told you about when we first met. At our next meeting I told you about angels. And now I will tell you of the greatest spirit of all, namely, GOD—the Being we pray to, the Being we speak of so often in the Church, the Being whose great name wicked people sometimes take in vain.

You must not think that I will try to tell you *every thing* about God. I could not do it if I wished, for I do not myself know every thing about him. Indeed, I know very little about him compared with what there is to be known—He is so great a being. But the little I do know is very important, and I will tell it to you just as a father brings home to his children a few grains of sand from the great sea-shore that winds all around the world.

God is like us in some things. Like us, he thinks, feels, chooses; and, like our

souls, he cannot be seen with our coarse
eyes.   But there are many things in which
he is very different from our spirits.   He
has no one body in which he lives.   No
voice of his goes ringing daily, and almost
every moment, through the air as our
voices do.   Our houses are sounding with
words from morning to night; the streets
and fields echo with calls and shouts and
talks; but these are *human* voices only.
Never once have we heard God's voice
among them.   We turn our ear upward,
and then downward; we set it toward
every part of the sky; we listen with all
our might for something that seems like
the voice of God.   But we hear nothing
but the whispering breeze, the humming
insects, and the talking or shouting men.
He speaks no words that we can hear.
God is always silent among us.   Years
come and go, life-times pass away, and it
is all the same—the same unbroken still-
ness.   You never heard God say any
thing; your fathers will tell you that they

never have heard the tones of his voice; your forefathers for hundreds of years will say as much. He *has* been known to speak on the earth; but the last time of his doing it, so far as we know, was more than eighteen hundred years ago. Then his voice fell from the sky, and some men said that it thundered. But now he is always silent.

Very different from us, also, is God in another thing. He can see and do things any distance away just as well as he can nigh. Your souls come and look out at your eyes, and see the things that are very near you quite plainly; but as soon as you begin to look a little way off every thing gets dim, and a little farther away you can see nothing at all. Your souls take hold of your hands and work easily on things your hands can reach, but on things miles away they cannot act at all. They have to send messengers. They have to shoot with the cannon. They have to stretch the telegraph wires. That is to say, they

have to make a *connection* in some way with
the thing to be acted on.   But it is not so
with God.   He can see things equally well
a thousand inches and a thousand miles
away—equally well where he is, and great
star-distances away where he is not.   He
can work on the most far-away things just
as well as he can on the nearest—just as
easily and quickly at the sun, or places in-
finitely farther off, as he can just here
where he happens to be.   Distance makes
no difference with his seeing or his doing.
A thousand millions of miles counts no
more than a foot.   It is all the same as if
he were every-where at once.

It takes some time for the arrow, though
shot from a strong bow strongly pulled, to
reach its mark.   It takes time for even the
sun to shoot its swift rays to us.   But
God can shoot his sight or his power to
the end of the universe in no time at all.
Before we can think it is there.   As soon
as it starts it reaches the end of its
journey.

Very much like this is another wonderful thing which you ought to think of. God is *always* seeing and doing. Much of the time we keep our eyes shut and see nothing at all. Much of the time we are tired and can do nothing. But God never sleeps, is never tired. There is no such thing as night to him. He keeps seeing and seeing, doing and doing, day and night, summer and winter, all the same.

No doubt it is hard for you to understand how all this can be, it is so unlike what you can do. And yet it is not unlike what your heart can do. How it goes on beating all the while, day and night, without ever resting or needing to rest a single moment. Yonder is a man eighty years old, and yet his heart has not once stopped beating since the day he was born, and it is not tired yet. God is like that heart; or rather, he is like the bright sun and stars that keep always moving and shining—never once stopping through all the ages, and yet as bright and fresh now as they were when men first saw them. Think of God as a great eye that is never tired of seeing. Think of him as a great hand that is never tired of working.

Another thing about God. He is *perfectly happy*. Men sometimes say that they are perfectly happy, but they do not mean what they say. There is always some drawback to their enjoyment, some bitter to their sweet, some sharp stones or thorns on the road they are traveling. And, taking months and years together, we all have something worse to speak of than enjoyments not quite so large and solid as they might be. We have pains, sorrows, sometimes miseries. But God is always as happy as he can be. 'Tis not with him as it is with us, now content and now discontented, now happy and now wretched—it is perfect bliss all the while. You have seen the sun when it had not a single spot or speck of cloud on its bright face. You have seen a spring of beautifully clear water, not merely half or quarter full but running over at the brim. You have seen our Connecticut not merely covering its bed, so that you could see no rocks nor patches of sand, but overflowing all its banks, so that all the low meadows around were covered. Well, such is the happiness of God—an unspotted sun, a full spring, an overflowing river.

The next thing I shall speak of is often thought very hard to be understood; but it is too important to be left out in telling about God. God is three. God is Father, Son, and Holy Spirit. The Son is he who was in Jesus Christ when he lived on the earth many centuries ago. The Holy Spirit is he who makes bad men good and good men better, especially in what you have heard called revivals of religion. Sometimes a great many persons in a place break off their sins and bad characters at the same time, and the Holy Spirit in their hearts is what persuades them to do it.

And the Father is he who sent the Son and sends the Holy Spirit. These three are all joined to each other in some way that we know nothing about, so as to make but one being, but one God. You must not think there are three Gods. This would be a very wrong and dangerous thought. There is but one God : only this one is Father, Son, and Holy Spirit, as closely joined together as are your three powers of thinking, feeling, and choosing. These three powers are not the same, but they are all equally great and honorable, and all belong to one soul. So the Father, Son, and Holy Spirit are not the same, but they are equally great and honorable, and together make one God.

A few years ago and there were no such things as your souls. They have but just begun to be. But there never was a time when there was no God. Go back in your thoughts as far as you can—go back hundreds of thousands of millions of years— and God was living then. Go back as

many times this great number of years as
there are specks of dust in the whole great
world we live on—God was living then.
He has *always* lived. He never had a beginning. What a thing to think of—
never a beginning, never a beginning!
You must try to get hold of this thought
so as to feel how great a difference there is
between God and us, who were just nothings only a few years ago. A being who
never began cannot but be. Nothing can
destroy him. He will go on living forever
and forever, and it will be because it will
not be possible for him to stop living.
Our souls, now that they have begun to
live, will always keep on living, (in this
respect they are like God,) but it will not
be because they cannot be made to die.
A plenty of power, such as I shall speak
of soon, could strike them out of being in
a moment more easily than you can lift a
finger. God has only to say in his heart,
Let them become nothings, and, quick as
a flash, our places would be empty. One

could never find us again, though he should
go hunting through all the worlds. That
word would be the last of us—quite
blotted out. But God cannot die. He is
such a being that he could no more be
made to die than two and two could be
made to be five. All the power in the
world or out of it, all the power you can
think of, cannot do such an impossible
thing.

When we began God made us. He
made us, and all things that we see, and
all things that are. Himself is the only
thing he did not make. All the fields and
waters and skies, all the plants and animals and men, all the dust itself which
they are made of, all the souls of men, all
the angels, all the matter and spirit that
have been, are, or shall be—you must look
to him as the Maker of all. What is of
most consequence to be remembered is
that he made *us*, bodies and souls—not
merely put us together, as a carpenter does
a house, but made the very materials which

he put together. Of course no man can do any thing like this. He cannot make the smallest bit of dust. He can make tools, machines, houses, that are really quite wonderful; but then he must have something to make his watches and locomotives and palaces out of. Who ever heard of a man making something out of nothing! This is what only God can do. Of course you cannot understand how he does it. Nobody understands this. But a great many things are true which we cannot explain, and this among others—that God made us and all other things out of just nothing. Hence he *owns* us and all things. No man has a right to think that he owns another man; no man has a right to think that he owns himself. God is the only owner of a man. He can fairly claim us and all that we call ours. If a man has a house to live in God made the carpenter that built it, the iron of the tools it was built with, and the wood it was built of. If a man has a farm or cattle or money,

God made those acres, even to the smallest atom of dust that is in them. He made the cattle and the grass that keeps them alive. He made the gold and silver deep in the mines, together with the fires that melted them and the hands that coined them. So we are his, and ours are his. The grown-up people and all they call theirs—they are his. The children and all they call theirs—they are his.

You have heard of great kings living gloriously in their palaces. Golden crowns are on their heads. Golden scepters are in their hands. They sit on thrones and wear robes that blaze with gold and precious stones. But the great thing is that such men are very powerful and can do almost any thing they choose with the people under them. Others look up to them with great admiration and say, May it please your majesties. Yet the greatest of these kings is not so great a king as God. They who know him best call him "King of kings," because he rules over all the kings of the world as well as over all other people. Heaven, where good angels live and where good men go when they die, is his glorious palace. There he reigns in glory over armies and armies beyond our counting—hosts whose greatest delight it is to have him reign over them. He reigns over all other worlds too—over all the stars you see in the sky as well as over the world on which we live. He gives laws to every thing about us. He tells *us* what we are to do, and he tells the stones, the trees, the winds, the waters, the lightnings, what they are to do. He has his shining servants who come and go at his bidding. He has his glittering armies that march and that fly. He has his court and his distant provinces. He has his rewards and punishments, his sword of justice and scepter of mercy. A great king is God, dwelling gloriously in heaven, his palace. Never such a king!

But it will not be of much use for us to remember that God is a great king unless we remember certain other things. One of them is this: From his glorious throne and palace in the sky God looks down and away and sees all that happens, day and night, in this world—all the great things and all the small things, all things done under the blaze of day and all things done under the blackness of night, all things that happen outside of a man and all things that happen inside of him. Nothing escapes the eye of God—not even the thoughts and feelings hidden deep within you and never yet put into words or even looks. Not a wish have you but God knows it as soon as you do. Are you about making up your minds to do something good or bad—God watches all your plans and motives as they by little and little take shape in you, and knows much more about them than you yourselves do. All your hopes and fears, all your pains and pleasures, all your works and plays, the smallest as well as the greatest of them, are at once plain as day to him. Take you never so much pains to be secret, he has already found you out. Get on as well as you may in hiding things from the prying eyes of parents and teachers, there is One from whom you cannot hide the smallest thing, no, not for one moment after it has come to be. Do not think that because heaven is so far away God cannot see you—his eye makes no account of distance. Do not think that because you are so small and your matters so small, God does not notice you and yours—his eye finds out the smallest things as well as the greatest. When a man wants to see something very far away he has to get what is called a telescope to help him, and even then he cannot see most of the things hidden in the distance. When a man wants to see something very small he has to put his eye to what is called a microscope, and even then, let him do his best, he cannot see but a small part of small things. But God needs no telescope to see far-off things, and all of them. He needs no microscope to see small things, and all of them. His eye out-travels all our glasses, and, though it be at the very ends of the universe, finds out every secret thing

God not only sees all that is passing every-where, but he can, without moving from his place in heaven, *do* with you and me and all things just as he pleases. Suppose he wants to make us great or small, sick or well, wise or foolish, unknown or famous, happy or miserable, he can do it in an instant. Suppose he wants to strike us into nothing or into the place where wicked angels are, he can do it in an instant. He has nothing to do but to will it. No strength nor cunning can prevent what he wills from coming to pass. You know that when *we* will to have any thing done that is very far from settling the matter. We have to follow up our willing with working, and, if we have to act at a distance, with traveling, and even then we are by no means sure of gaining our ob-

ject. But, with God, to will and to do
are the same thing. Just as soon as he
decides that a thing shall at once be, at
once it is. The willing begins and ends
the whole matter. Should we try to re-
sist him that would make no difference.
Should all the world come to our help, and
all the angels besides, it would make no
difference. God's will and power, from
away where he sits throned in the sky,
would conquer us in an instant. God is
ALMIGHTY.

Yet for all that God is so strong, able
to do in an instant just what he pleases,
able to do all things, he never does any
thing wrong. This is a beautiful fact—
the other was a grand one. Both beautiful and grand is it to know that God never
makes a bad use of his wonderful power,
that no foolish nor bad thing is ever done
by him. We need not fear his treating us
worse than we deserve through either mistake or cruelty. This is very comforting.
It is beautiful to see at least one being the

white robes of whose life have no spot
upon them.

Never doing any thing wrong himself,
he does not like to have others do wrong.
He is displeased with us when we do so.
Seeing all you do, whether done by day or
night, whether without your body or
within your soul, if he sees you doing what
you ought not, be sure he is offended at
you. And if you keep on doing badly he
will not stop at being offended. He will
go on to punish you. And he can go very
far in the way of punishing. If we will
not be persuaded to cease doing evil and
to learn doing well, he will at last shut us
in with those wicked angels, of whom I
have told you, in their dreadful world.
Above all things let us be careful not to
come to this. Better to have any thing
else happen to us!

Though God is so displeased, and at last
so stern, with those who do wickedly, you
must not suppose that he is a harsh and
cruel being. This would be doing him

great injustice, for really he is the most patient and loving of beings. Your fathers and mothers, however much they may love you, have no heart at all compared with God. Though we are great sinners against him, he is giving us all the while millions on millions of good things, in fact all the fair and pleasant things we have, to make us comfortable and happy in this world. He has sent us a Book from heaven to tell us how to be good and happy forever. He has come himself to shed his own blood and life to take away our sins, if we will be sorry for them. Every day he sends the Holy Spirit to try to make us good, and does not give it up though the treatment he gets is very far from what it should be. By every means he is trying to take you and us all to live with him forever in the glorious heaven where he reigns. This is what he would love to do. His heart is in this. He threatens and punishes only because he must do so to keep wickedness from filling the world.

This is the great and good Being to
whom we pray.   This is he whom we worship and preach about in the churches.
This is he of whom your teachers in the
Sunday-school, and I hope your parents at
home, tell you.   It is the same being you
read of in the Bible and many other good
books, and whom good people every-where
worship and love and fear and obey.   And,
do you know, I should never have thought
of preaching to you about God had I not
wanted to persuade you to fear and love
and serve him also.   Such a great and
good being—one who never himself began
to be, but from whom all other things began—one who sits in heaven as a glorious
king, and from thence sees all that happens and all that you do, and is so strong
and knowing that he can, without stirring
from his place, do with you and all things
just as he pleases—one who never does
wrong himself and does not like to have
others do it—who is patient and loving
and pitiful beyond measure, and tries ever

to make us fit for heaven and then take us there—this is a being none of us can afford to displease, and whom it ought to be easy for us to love and serve. It is easy for you to do it, now that you are young—easy compared with what it will be by and by. By and by it will be very hard. Now is the time to make the great God your friend and father. I hope you will not fail to do it, and will grow up not like many who forget him and break his holy laws and become miserable forever, but to love him as your best friend and try to do all things that please him, and so at last go to live with him in glory everlasting in heaven.

I saw two little boys. They lived in the same place, were of nearly the same age, dressed much alike, and played together. One day they both stood where two ways met, and one said, I will go this way, and the other said, I will take the other. So they parted. For a while they were so near each other that they could talk together, but soon they went too far apart for this, and then they lost sight of each other. But I could see them still, and I saw that the path on which one boy was going kept creeping up, and was all the while getting brighter and pleasanter, while that on which the other was going kept creeping down, and was all the while getting darker and drearier. At last it grew hard to see, so I took a spy-glass and kept on watching. And at last I saw him on the rising path get up so high and become so bright that he seemed almost like a star, and then I saw him go in at the gates of a beautiful city. Then I turned to watch the other boy, and I watched him going down till at last he seemed at the bottom of a deep pit, and his clothes were all rags, and his face looked so wicked and O so sad! so sad it made my heart ache. Then came a flash where he stood. I never saw him again. And this was the child who took to sinful ways. The other set out to love and serve God, and God took him.

IV.

THE EMPIRE OF GOD.

AN empire is a large region ruled over by a king or emperor.

Sometimes an empire is *very* large, including many countries that stretch along for thousands of miles. Such is the Russian empire. One almost gets tired at the mere idea of traveling about such immense coasts, across such immense plains and mountains and seas, over so many millions on millions of square miles of land and water as belong to this very large empire.

But I am now to tell about an empire still larger than this, and far larger than any other the world ever saw. It is that great territory over which God rules as king. No other realm like this. The sun never shone on one so broad and grand.

By the side of it all other empires that we see or read of, if put together, would be of no account.

For see. All other empires are only *parts* of this. All our world belongs to it. All the American countries, north and south—all the countries of the Old World away to the sunrising—all the islands, great and small, that dot the ocean for twenty-four thousand miles—all the oceans themselves, that no nations pretend to own—all belong to this one great empire of God. Republics, monarchies, deserts— called by this name and by that, claimed by this nation and by that, inhabited or uninhabited—heathen lands that know not God as well as those lands where he is worshiped and served—they all belong to this heavenly empire. What a great empire it is !

But great as is the empire which all the countries and seas of the world make, they are but a small part of the empire over which God reigns. Look up at the sky some bright night. You see it all sown with stars. If you could go toward almost any one of these stars, swift as the lightning, for thousands of years, you would on coming to it find it a much larger world than this on which we live. We can see some twenty millions of such worlds in a fair night, and each of them has about it a family of many other worlds which we cannot see at all. And there is not one of them which, if we should go to it and question it, would fail to confess that it belongs to God. He is its king. He owns and rules it. It is one of the many countries of his empire.

Is this the end? Have we found the last countries ruled over by God? If we go farther shall we come to the territory of *another* king—come to other worlds which God does not own or to no territories at all? Do not think it. Could you stand on the most distant world that we can see, you would see just as many and distant worlds beyond you as you do now;

and if from that point you should travel on again as far as to the last twinkling star it would be all the same; and so on forever, for aught I know. Wherever you found a world you would find it belonging to the empire of God. And should you ever come to an end of worlds you would never come to the end of that great sky in which the worlds are moving about like floating islands in a shoreless ocean. And this shoreless sky itself belongs to God. Empty space is as much his as are the solid worlds. No part of it which he does not own and rule. He sees it. His power is there. At any time he chooses he can make it shine with matter and swarm with life.

Of course you will feel that this is a wonderfully great empire. What line could go around it? What ship could sail across it? What map could give all its provinces, far and near? What lightning on its fiery path could ever come in sight of the end? No boundaries, no neighbors, nothing beyond it—the sum total of all things—behold the empire of God!

And about as populous with living beings as it is vast. The air, the seas, the lands of our world, are alive with animals of almost innumerable forms. What multitudes of men now living! What hosts of men who did live on the earth, and whose souls when they went away went *somewhere*, and are living to-day somewhere in the empire of God as truly as they ever did! And then think of the many, many beings there must be in the untold millions of other worlds that we know of! I should be sorry to be put at counting them. I would sooner undertake to count all the leaves on the trees and all the sands on the shores. Yes, I would rather try to do this than to reckon up all the *spirits* even that are to be found in all the stretches of space. The population of India or China astonishes us—that of God's whole empire would confound us and take our breath away. Nations num-

berless, races on races without end, mighty
populations added to mighty populations,
till our strongest thought staggers and
falls under the burden! Once in ten
years men go round all our country and
count up all 'the people. The *census* we
say is taken, and we stand astonished in
the presence of forty millions of people.
But not even the angels could take the
census of God's empire. Suppose the
swiftest of them should go forth and
sweep in every direction on their mighty
pinions, counting, counting, counting—I
tell you their wings would droop before
finishing a single corner of the empire.
That census could not be taken—no, not
even by the Gabriels. God himself alone
can number all his subjects.

A country may be very large and yet
be very poor. It may be a Siberia—little
more than rocks and ice-fields. It may be
a Sahara—little more than burning sands.
But not far away is another great country
of a very different sort. It is naturally

full of all sorts of valuable things. It has rich soils, delightful climates, fat pastures, tempting grain-fields, fruits and plants of ten thousand useful kinds, founts, streams, rivers, lakes every-where, great forests, productive fisheries, endless mines of coal and iron and silver and gold, sublime mountains, lovely vales, sweet home-sites without number—in a word, as we say, it is a country of " vast resources." Its people are proud of it. Its orators boast of it. Its friends look at it and are glad ; its enemies look at it and are afraid—so full is it, in air and water and land, of what goes to make a great and powerful empire.

But there is an empire still richer. It includes the rich country I have just spoken of and many such countries besides. In it are all the rich farms of the world, all its earldoms, dukedoms, principalities ; all the palaces, treasuries, armies, fleets of kings and emperors ; all the useful things and splendid things that sleep in the bosom of seas or bosom of land ; all arts, manufactures, civilizations; all the might and speed that hide in winds and waters and fires and lightnings and earthquakes and magnetisms and gravities and glorious sweep of suns and stars; all the strength of the strong, the wisdom of the wise, the courage of the brave, the beauty of the beautiful, the riches of the rich, the influence of the influential, the goodness of the good, and ten thousand other sorts of wealth and power not to be found in this world—all belong to the empire of God. Suns and stars, with all their strange and glorious treasures, are in it. Heaven itself is in it. The infinite power and knowledge of God are every-where in it—to do all things that need to be done. Was ever so rich an empire? No end to its stores and resources! Mountains of them as high as heaven! Oceans of them broad and deep as the sky! Did you ever see the like? We lift up both hands in amazement. Such an empire can stand the strain of endless wars. It can afford to laugh at the idea of being *exhausted.* Indeed, its resources can never become less—what goes out here comes back there; what disappears there reappears yonder in the same or in some other form.

Houses sometimes so shine in the sunbeams that it is painful to look at them. I have seen cities on sunny hill-sides so lit up with noon-day splendors that at a distance they looked like cities on fire. And I have known, and in part seen, a great *empire* even more glittering than glittering Genoa and Naples at their brightest—as glittering as the stars by night or as the sun himself by day. In fact, the sun and stars are only a dimmer part of this empire. What floods of brightness from our summer sun! It dazzles, it blinds—we turn away our eyes in self-defense. But all the stars are just as bright—being themselves true suns with their glory somewhat lessened to us by distance. And even our earth, which often looks to us so dull and dark, if seen from afar would

shine like the queenly moon or the bright
evening-star. So it is with that part of
the empire which we see, and so, no doubt,
it is with that part of it which we do not
see because so far away. All sparkles.
The light covers all like royal robes. Re-
motest provinces flash like gems. Some
districts flame and dazzle more than noon-
day suns. Spangles beyond counting,
lamps without end, immense diamond-fields
whose untold diamonds shine through,
cities on cities all round the sky whose
every window is blazing, as if for a vic-
tory, with every possible color—such are
even the frontiers of the glorious empire
of God. Such, I say, are the *frontiers.*
But if we could only see the capital—the
London or Rome of this great empire,
that central region we have learned to call
Heaven—how dark all the rest would seem
by the side of that wonderful shining
which is " like unto a stone most precious,
even like a jasper stone, clear as crystal,
having the glory of God ! "

This most brilliant of empires is naturally the most famous of empires. There
are some realms of which men only faintly
hear. Once heard of, they scarcely get a
second thought. No account is made of
them. They are hardly more than names.
History turns them off with a paragraph
or a sentence. Perhaps the sentence is
almost or quite a sneer. But then history
has also her famous empires—empires
much in the thoughts and on the lips of
men, and to which, for some reason, men
look up with great respect and admiration.
Such was the Roman empire. Such were
the empires of Alexander and Charlemagne
and Napoleon. These made a great figure
in their day. Almost everybody has
heard of them. Their names are still
sounding in the world like trumpets.
When people talk of "glory" they are
very apt to be thinking about the famous
empires that raised a great wave in the
world's affairs in their time, and which
wave is running yet.

But see an empire more famous still. Who has not heard of the empire of the Creator? Who has not heard great things of it—heard the *very* greatest and sublimest things of it? Not a corner of the universe where it is not known. Not a language within the great round of the heavens which does not speak of it with wonder. As for *our* corner, this little earth on which we live, all its religions are full of the idea, more or less vailed, of a Divine government. Men's consciences are full of it. Much more the Bible—a book read in more than a hundred languages, spoken weekly in thousands of churches, and studied daily in millions of homes. And not in vain. The world rings with the fame of the empire. It is spoken to in endless prayers. It is praised in ceaseless hymns. And the great praising music swells louder and louder from age to age. Never was empire so much on the lips and in the thoughts of men—especially of wise and good men. They

believe glorious things of it. To them it
has a mighty history. To them it is play-
ing a sublime part. To them it shows a
sublime procession of events all its own—
kings and queens and great captains clad
in purple and gold. Behold creations,
miracles, prophecies, revelations, regenera-
tions, salvations—see God in form of man,
Jesus dying on the cross, sinners purified
and forgiven, ascending to heaven—see
glorious objects, glorious wars, glorious
victories, glorious fruits of victories!
Never did empire spread such banners—
never did such armies march beneath!
As to what it is, what it has done, what
.it aims to do, what it certainly will do,
this empire has no equal. It is the joy
and trust and hope and love, as well as
fear, of all the best of mankind. Their
hearts build to it monuments high as
heaven. Their hearts raise to it triumph-
al arches that can span the sky. And yet
this empire of God is not thought as much
of and celebrated as splendidly here as it

is in most worlds. So *I* think. I *know* that there is one immense country—so immense as to easily balance all the rest of the universe—which is always ringing, from one end of it to the other, with the praise of the King eternal, immortal, invisible; and it almost seems as if I could hear at this moment a voice pouring down through the. sky as the voice of many waters, and as the voice of a great thunder, and as the voice of harpers harping with their harps, saying, "Amen; blessing and glory and thanksgiving and honor and might and power be to Him that sitteth on the throne for ever and ever."

This famous empire is very old. Who can tell how old it is? Not I nor any other man. I can easily tell how old the British empire is, and the German, and I am sure that not an empire in the world and of the world goes back six thousand years. But who knows when the empire of God began, or can tell a time when it was not? Of course there was no beginning whatever to that shoreless ocean of space in which swim the worlds as so many round, shining islands. The region itself has always existed, has always been full of the sight and power of God, and so has always been an empire of his. But there must have been a time when it was an *empty* empire—empty of every thing but its eternal King. There came a time when worlds began to roll and shine in it—when the *first* world started off on its golden round. When was that? I cannot tell. Perhaps no angel, even, can tell. But it must have been a very distant time—much farther back than the founding of any other empire of which we know. Learned men will tell you that our world must have been rolling for millions of years. And, for one, I have no doubt that worlds beyond counting are even older still—that it would be almost like counting eternity to count the years which have come and gone since untold stars began to twinkle in the sky at the bidding of the Creator. What a glorious antiquity! How the little earthly empires that so loudly boast of their few centuries—how infant-like they look in the venerable presence of such an empire as this!

This empire, old as it is, has never had but one King. People think it something to tell of if the same *family* (father, son, grandson, and so on) manages to hold the same throne for a few hundred years. Kings die like other people. Indeed, they are apt to die sooner than some who lead quieter and less tempted lives. Forty or fifty years at the outside take away the healthiest of them. Then comes his successor, and, before long, another successor. And, after awhile, the royal *family* itself dies out, or is set aside for another. What is called a new dynasty begins to reign. So it has happened over and over again in France and other countries. So it is liable to happen at any moment in any empire the sun shines on.

But one empire has never changed its

dynasty, or even its sovereign. Old as it is, almost making us afraid with the mighty tale of its years, it has always had the same King. No successor has even been thought of. You will never hear of a new reign in this wide realm. Coronation Day will never come twice here. " God save the King " always means the same Person. Some of us are very glad that we do not have to see every now and then a regency, or a new election. God will never die. He will never resign in favor of some other. He will never throw up his kingly power in weariness and disgust, as some kings have done. But on, steadily on, will his reign proceed. The latest ages will see him on the throne as ever. From Everlasting to Everlasting is his name. I am glad of it. This is the King for me. I want no other. No other could begin to do as well. No better news can come to me than that the great and good God, the wisest and best and strongest of beings, will wear his crown forever. Such good news *has* come to me. "Rejoice ye heaven, and let the earth be glad; for the Lord God Omnipotent *always* reigneth." No danger that you will some day (some night, rather) wake up to find the Great Throne vacant or filled by a new sovereign. Suppose the worlds should some time hear through all their shining fleets the voice of a mighty angel proclaiming God to be dead—what a shock! Deliver us from this whatever may happen! We *shall* be delivered from it. All who come after us will be delivered from it. Not an insect need tremble in its sunbeam, not a star nor soul need tremble in its orbit lest the empire fall into new hands. Go calmly and brightly on, all ye worlds; that last and worst of calamities will be spared you. "God sitteth king *forever*."

I have seen empires shake. I have seen them fall, time and again. And O how many, many, shaking, trembling, falling empires have been seen by those who have gone before me, away back to the beginning! The very ruins of some that were once famous and vast can hardly be found. History can count up not a few memorable examples. And I fully expect that before a great while some empires that now make much show in the world will shake as a tree does when a mighty wind gets hold of its branches and wrestles with them. They will strain and bow and fall headlong, as did the empires of Alexander and the Cæsars. There is not an empire on this globe that is *sure* to be here ten years hence—I might as well have said ten *days* hence. A single day, between dawn and dark, has laid low many a kingdom, and is likely to do it again. Not a kingdom on earth but is sure to fall some day, strong as it may now seem. In one way or another, at one time or another, down it will come, never to rise again. Nothing but its name will be left—perhaps not even that. Alas! these trembling, falling things—human empires!

7

But cheer up, for I will now show you an empire that knows how to stand. No enemies will ever be able to smite it to the ground. It will never become so old and feeble as to fall of itself, like some old tree that has filled out its time, gradually grown rotten at heart and dry in branch, till at last a breath of wind or the weight of a bird tumbles it to the ground. From age to age it will stand mightily against time, mightily against rebellious men, mightily against even the rebellious angels with Satan at their head. It *never* will fall—no, never! no, never! It never will be in the least danger of falling. Nothing will ever even make it tremble, or give it a single little jar such as would shake a dew-drop from its leaf. Of what other empire can this be said? How glad I am that there is one country that can be counted on—one great empire that will stand unmoved and immovable all the long ages of eternity through! I like to see something that is not liable any moment to come down into the dust, something to anchor safely by, something that can neither burn nor drown nor decay, nor be smitten into ruins or even into danger —firmest of pyramids, with the whole creation for its base! One feels stronger and safer even to *see* such an everlasting, immovable thing—especially in this world where winds and waves and earthquakes and steady blows of Time's great hammer bring, sooner or later, every thing else into the dust.

One, two, three—perhaps I have known as many well-governed countries. One, two, thirty—certainly I have known as many countries ill-governed. Sometimes empires are woefully mismanaged. Disorder reigns. There are no steady laws or the laws are bad. The people are not cared for—the sheep have no shepherd. " No shepherd," do I say? The shepherd is a wolf. He watches, he tears, he devours. The people are robbed. The people are treated like slaves. The throne and palace glitter, the subjects groan and starve. Taxes, taxes, taxes—without measure and without end! Blood, blood, blood—scaffolds for the great and halters for the small! Passed over from the great tyrant to lesser tyrants, then from the lesser to the least, by successive turns of the screw, through all the grades of wicked officers, the juices of the nation's life are squeezed out. Nothing but dry pumice is left. This is the way some empires have been governed. Be thankful, children, that you were not born in any such empire, but in a very different one—the *Empire of God*.

For this empire, vast as it is, is governed in a most noble and magnificent way. Nay, it is governed in a way that has never been equaled—in a way that never *can* be equaled—for it is a perfect way. You must consider that God, who governs this huge empire, is almighty and all-wise and all-good. This means that his intentions are the best possible. This means that he makes no mistakes. This means

that he can do all that power can do. So
it means that the whole vast country, away
through all the stars, is kept in the best
possible order. Its vastness does not stand
in the way of this. No Turkish empire is
this—a few central provinces well kept
under, but as one goes away from the capital disorder ever increasing, until at last,
on the frontiers, the government amounts
to nothing. The most remote provinces of
God's empire are as well cared for and
regulated as the most central. All parts
are thoroughly watched over, day and
night. Not a soul, not a worm, escapes
notice. Each is cared for with an interest
and zeal that never flag. The smallest beginnings of wrong things are at once noticed and put under checks. The smallest
beginnings of right things are at once noticed and put under helps. The King
knows just what to do to meet each case,
and he always does the right thing at the
right moment. So it happens that there is
no other empire anywhere that is so capi-

tally governed as this. Of course such things as plants, waters, winds, worlds, always do just as their Maker wishes to have them. He never has to find fault with them. But among *spirits* there is some disobedience, (much in this world and at least one other,) but it is always found out, stopped, or properly punished. You see there may be a splendid government over bad persons. However, I think that this government of God is so nobly managed that in most places in his empire there is no disobedience at all, but the people always do in all respects just as they ought. No doubt all such places are bright and happy. They are gardens. They are beautiful as sunsets. They are as beautiful as the lovely characters and lives that dwell in them. And, by and by, those parts of the empire which are now disturbed by wrong-doers will all be quieted, and the wrong-doers themselves will either become good-doers or will be shut up where they can do no more harm.

V.

THE LAWS OF GOD.

IF you should go into some men's houses you would see long rows of books with white leather covers, and if you should ask what sort of books they are, you would be told that they are law-books. And what are law-books? Why, they are books that tell what *must* be done. The people get together and choose a number of men to go to Washington and there talk over what it would be best for people to do, and when they have made up their minds they print what they want in newspapers and books, and bid the people do it. If anybody will not do it he shall be fined, or put in prison, or some other disagreeable thing shall be done to him. These printed sayings are called *laws*.

But printed laws are not the only ones.

By degrees men have fallen into the way
of calling almost any thing a law that
shows what a person wishes and also has a
must with it. Now you know that there
are a great many things besides printed
paper that can do this. A mere look or
motion of the hand can do it. When
your father looks at you in a certain way,
though he says not a word, you know that
he means that you are to be silent, and
that you *must* be. When your teacher
points his finger at you as you sit in school,
though he says nothing, you know that he
means that you are not to move about so
much, and that you *must* not. When,
some time, your father brings you a letter,
you know at once that you are to carry it
to the post-office, and that you must not
dream of doing otherwise, though he does
not so much as open his lips; or if at a
quarter past nine o'clock in the morning
he silently puts your school-books in your
hand, you know that you are to start off
at once for school and *must* do so. Now,

such things show what your parents and teachers and others want to have done, and mean to have you do, just as plainly as any printed paper could· do it. So people have fallen into the way, and very properly, as I think, of calling very many things of this sort " commands " and " laws."

I will now tell you something about the laws of that great Being of whom I was lately speaking to you, whose name is God.

And, first, there are the laws which God has given to such things as have no soul —to such things as the sun, moon, and stars; as stones, grass, flowers, and trees; as insects, fishes, birds, and oxen. People sometimes call them natural laws. God made each of these soulless things for a good purpose, and so he put in each something to show what he wanted it to be and do, and with it he put a *must*. It is all one as though he had said to the star, " Star, your business is to shine, and shine you *must!*" to the tree, "Tree, your business is to give shade and beauty and fruit and fuel, and I bid you do it!" to the cattle, "Cattle, your business is to work for and feed man, and I command you to do it!" There is something in the make of each of these things that shows us, when we look carefully at it, that God meant all this in regard to it. In short, he has put his *law* into it to make it be and do what he pleases. He has put his law into the bee to make it build its comb and gather its honey, into the bird to make it fly in the air, into the fish to make it swim in the water, into the ox to make it walk and work on the land.

This sort of God's laws is given not only to such senseless and brute things as I have mentioned, but also to men, to you and me, and indeed to every thing God has made. He has so made your bodies that unless you do so and so they will be sick—that unless you do so and so they will not grow properly, but become weak, crooked, and painful. He has so made your minds that unless they have a plenty to do they will be unhappy—that unless they get knowledge, and practice well at trying to use it, they will never become strong and able to do much in the world. When we see how *you* are made it is very plain that God wants you to do a hundred things that might be mentioned, and also very plain that there is a *must* about it; if you will not do them he means, and means that you shall understand, that you will have to suffer. Now the things in you that show all this are God's natural laws. You are bound to learn and obey them, just as though he had sent them to you printed on paper. Things that have not souls, for the most part, obey this sort of laws very well; they cannot do otherwise, the *must* is so strong upon them. But such beings as we are can largely disobey; but in that case we still do wrong, and will have to suffer for it. Not a few people have an idea that they can break this kind of God's laws without any sin, but it is not so. And it is well for people to begin to feel while they are children that it is not so, and to act accordingly. If *you* will begin now to be very careful in obeying God's natural laws it will save you a great many troubles and aches, and perhaps will save you from early graves.

But besides these laws of God there is another kind which senseless and brute things do not have, called the *laws of con-science.* These belong only to such things as have spirits, as men and angels. Some-thing within us, which God put there, tells us what is right and wrong, what things we ought to do and ought not to do, and if we will not do what it says it punishes us. Have you never felt it? Have you not felt something within telling you that you must not do such and such things be-cause they would be wrong, and then when you have done them have you not felt very unhappy? Well, that something within you is conscience. Its laws are God's laws. They tell you what God wants you to do, and that you *must* do it or be unhappy. God put them in you for this very purpose. He does not give this sort of laws to stones, and trees, and birds, and oxen—they have no notion of right and wrong. It is only beings like you who have souls who have the ideas of *ought* and *ought not*. You are having such ideas all the while. Every few minutes you are feeling that it would not be right to do this and would be right to do that, and are feeling badly or pleasantly according as you do the one or the other. At any time when you think about such things your heart will tell you that it is wrong to tell falsehoods, to take things that do not belong to you, to disobey your parents, to be quarrelsome, to be idle and mischievous and wasteful and unthankful, and so on. Now you must remember that when you hear your heart telling you such things you are hearing God's laws. He has put them into your heart to show you what he

wants you to do, and he says, *You must*
with each of them.   The unpleasant feeling
which you know you will have unless you
do as he says is a part of this *must.*

There is one thing about the laws of
God in your heart which, perhaps, I ought
not to fail to tell you of now, it is so very
important for young people to know and
act on it as early as they can.   This is
that, unless one is careful, these laws very
easily get faded, blurred, rubbed out.
Suppose one of you should go from home
a long distance to school and his father
should write him a letter telling him how
he must behave, what books he must
study, what clothes he must wear.   Now
if this boy should take no care of this
letter, but let it lie about on the floor, in
the dust, on chairs, benches, the ground, as
might happen—rubbed against as chance
would have it by any and every thing—
what would be the consequence?   Why,
the writing would get so faded and soiled
that it would be a hard matter to read it,

and an easy matter to read it wrongly. After a little while, though the writing was beautifully plain at first, it would be hard to spell out what the wishes of that father were, and very likely great mistakes would be made, and the father made to say things that he never intended to say. That little word " *not* " rubbed out would change his whole meaning. This will help you to understand how, if you are careless about your conscience and God's laws written on it, you will after awhile have them less plain than they now are—will have them faded, blurred, possibly quite rubbed out, and may make great and dreadful mistakes in trying to read them. I assure you that such things often happen. So you must take great care of your consciences. You must not handle them roughly. You must not let soiled and soiling things come much against them. You must treat them as people do a beautiful picture made on the finest of paper— they set it in a gold frame, they cover it

with glass, they hang it up in the neatest
and best room they have, and go in with
their friends to see, admire, and study it
as often as they can.

But besides these laws of God written
in consciences and hearts, there is still another kind nearly as much brighter,
plainer, and nobler than these as these
are brighter and nobler than the kind I
first mentioned, and which are given to
stones and other senseless and brutal
things. Can you not think what this still
better kind is? What is that which tells
us what we ought to do and must do in
plainer words, in brighter and more heavenly words, than our own hearts and consciences ever use? What *Book* is that
which good people love and honor so much
as having come down to us out of heaven
to tell us about God and what he wants
us to do? You see I am now speaking
of the BIBLE—of God's laws in the Bible.
The Bible is a *law*-book. It tells us what
God wants us to do—what he says we

must do—what he says we must do or be punished severely. If we do what it says he will take us to heaven, that most beautiful of all places, where he himself lives; if not, he will send us to that most wretched of all places where live the evil angels.

The Bible is full of the strongest kind of laws, and its *must* is of the strongest kind. Some of its laws are the same that conscience gives us, but many of them are quite new, such as conscience says nothing about. Thus, it says that you must not tell untruths, nor steal, nor disobey your parents, nor be idle and mischievous and quarrelsome and unthankful, just as your own hearts do, (only the tone and the words are much stronger and swifter, and the *must* a great deal louder and more terrible,) but then it says very much more than this; for example, that you must keep one day in the week holy, that you must love the Lord Jesus Christ, and do your best to please him, and pray

to God in his name, and ask pardon of
your sins for his sake, and do many other
things besides which your own hearts tell
you nothing about.

The first kind of God's laws is given
to all things, of all kinds, in all places;
the second kind, the laws of conscience,
are given only to things that have souls,
as men and angels; this third kind of
which we have just been speaking, the
laws of the Bible, are as yet given to
a still smaller number of men, though
God means that sooner or later it shall be
given to the whole world. He means to
have it done, and he means to have good
people do it. If you live he will want
you to help by giving money and in other
ways. To be sure all persons all over the
world have the laws of conscience, and,
if they would, they could get along with
these, and get to heaven at last without
any Bible-laws; but they *will* not. People do not pay much attention to conscience where they have no Bible. In this

world Bible-laws and conscience-laws work
best together.   And   then the Bible is the
greater light of the two.   Have you not
seen a little candle, not much larger than
your finger, the wick all loaded with the
black, choking snuff, sending out so poor
a light that hardly any thing could be
seen at the back of the room ?   Well, this
is like many a conscience.   But the Bible
is like the sun, shining brightly, shining
far, flooding all things with light, making
the waters glisten like silver, the mountains burn, the valleys smile, and all things
above ground through half the world
stand out to view in beautiful clearness.
The candle is very useful where the sun
cannot be had—it is very useful even
when the sun is shining for the purpose
of going down into cellars and searching
out dark corners ; but after all, you know,
the sun is the great thing, and very unfortunate is the man who has to do without
it. So, very unfortunate are those who
have no sun-Bible to light them—nothing

but a candle-conscience, which indeed is very well in its place, but, after all, is nothing but a candle.

Is the Bible God's glorious book of laws? Then the youngest child among you can see how it ought to be treated. Very respectfully, no doubt, more so than you would treat the greatest man in the world in case you should happen to meet him; very studiously, no doubt, more so than you would any book that you are set to learn from in your schools or that wise men have written. Is it strange that Sabbath-schools should be started to teach it to you, that ministers should take so much pains to explain and preach it every Sunday, and that there should be great societies kept up by much giving and working of good people in order to print it and send it cheaply into all parts of the world? There is not another such book anywhere. It is the Book of books. We could do without all other books better than we could without this. You have sometimes seen it bound in beautiful and costly leather, its leaves edged with gold, and perhaps pictured bars of silver or gold fastening up the delicate white leaves, and did you never think that never did book as well deserve so splendid a dress, and that the grand outside is but in keeping with the precious and heavenly laws found within? So you *should* think.

I have but one other kind of God's laws to speak to you about. These are such laws as those who live in heaven get *directly* from God. The holy dead and the angels are with God. They see him and hear him, and get laws directly from his own lips. With his own voice he tells them what he wants them to do, the holy errands on which he wishes them to fly, the noble things he would have them do, far or near, for him, for people in this and other worlds, for themselves. But you ask, Is there any *must* about all this, any *must* in heaven? How can one be perfectly happy with a *must* sounding in his ears? Yes, there is law even in heaven. Every angel and saint there knows that he cannot stay there unless he keeps good, and keeps doing as God wishes to have him. He knows that the first thing he should do contrary to God's will would drive him out of that holy place as swift as the lightning's flash. So all God's wishes in heaven have a mighty *must* at the end of them. They are, in fact, God's *laws*, as I have said. Now, in this world, though we have a good many of God's laws and several kinds of them, as you have seen, yet we have none of just this kind. God now never deals directly with living people, however good they may be. They never see him nor hear him. He never even sends an angel or a word of his own handwriting to them. Once it was not so. A great while ago he sometimes talked with a man face to face, as a man talks with his friend. Twice he wrote off some laws with his own finger on two

tables of stone, and sent them to a nation.
Once he came down on a mountain in
thunders and lightnings and earthquakes,
and, with an awful voice that made people
tremble as if they would die, spoke all
the Ten Commandments to millions of
people at once in one great congregation.
Once he took a body such as we have and
a voice like ours, and lived among men
thirty-three years, teaching them and com-
manding them with his own lips such
things as he wished them to know and
do. And a great many, many times he
has sent angels with their swift snow-white
wings and glorious forms and faces to bring
his laws to men. But all this was long
ago. He never does such things now.
The only laws we shall ever get from him
as long as we live will be natural laws,
conscience laws, and Bible laws; but if in
this world we try honestly to go according
to these laws and trust in Christ, in the
next world we shall have the other kind
also to go by. There are millions and

millions of children now in heaven who
get laws from God's own mouth, and you
will one day do the same if you now love
and serve Christ according to what you
know. And you need not be troubled
about that *must;* that will belong to even
these higher laws of heaven as it does to all
others that God gives us. It will be no
trouble to you should you ever get to
heaven. It will not make you feel as if
tied up, forced, slaved. But you will feel
glad that neither you nor anybody else
will be *allowed* to turn heaven into a
wicked place, you will so hate all sorts of
wickedness.

Now I have but a few more things to
say. One is, that all these laws, of whatever kind, that God gives, whether natural
laws or conscience laws or Bible laws or
heaven laws, have not the least speck of
wrong or fault about them: every one of
them is beautifully and gloriously wise
and good, and meant to do us good. The
laws that men make are apt to have much

that is bad about them, and not a few of them are all badness from beginning to end, and the more one minds them the worse off he is. But it is not so with any of God's laws.

Another thing I wish to say is, that minding one kind of these laws will help you to mind all the rest. Thus, if you mind those laws which I first told you about, called natural laws, it will help you to do what your consciences bid you do; and if you mind your consciences it will help you to do what your Bibles bid you do; and if you mind your Bibles it will help you to do what God will bid you do in heaven, speaking to you face to face. Indeed, if you go by your consciences you are sure to go by the Bible, and if you go by both of these you are sure at last to go by such laws as they have in heaven.

The last thing I have to say is, that the better and longer you go according to any of these kinds of God's laws the pleasanter you will find it and the better you

will be. It is not so with many laws I
could tell you of. It is not so with many
of the laws that men make. Above all,
it is not so with *any* of the laws that Satan, your great enemy and mine, makes.
The more you do as he wants to have you
the more dissatisfied and the worse you
will be. You will be the most wretched
and the most wicked when you obey him
the most. If you want to be perfectly
wretched and perfectly wicked you have
only to obey him perfectly. On the other
hand, if you would be perfectly happy
and perfectly good you have only to obey
God, your great Friend and Father, perfectly. Which will you try to do? A
great many children are just now making
wise answer to this question, and are set-
ting out toward heaven. I hope you will
be *sure* to join this bright army. They
are bright and fair now as their feet pat-
ter on, and their fresh young faces look
up toward the glory that streams down
from the heavenly hills; but the bright

faces will be brighter by and by, when they get nearer the glory. At last they will go in at the dazzling gates of the city whose streets are paved with gold. May *every one* of you be among them!

VI.

THE WORD OF GOD.

I LATELY told you of God's laws, which God has given his creatures to tell them what they *must* do. I then said that these laws are found most plainly and fully in the book we call the Bible.

The word Bible means *book*. This book is so called because it is *the* Book, the Book of books, the best book in the world. And I hope that you will feel that it is really all this when I have finished telling you certain things about it.

The first of these things is that God made the Bible. Men make the paper on which it is printed, men do the printing and binding, men carry it all around the world to sell or give away; but the thoughts in the Bible, and the way these thoughts are put together, and the words which carry them, all came first from God. He told holy men what to write and how to write it—sometimes by a great voice mid thunders and lightnings, sometimes by angels, and sometimes as by whispers to the thoughts. And they wrote just what he wanted to have written, in just the way he wanted it written. But people must have something to show that it was so, and so God gave these writers power to work miracles and speak prophecies. They cured sick people by a word, divided rivers, put storms to rest, called down fire from heaven, raised the dead. Of course reasonable men who saw such things done could not well help believing. And they copied and spread the writings they believed in, and at last printed, and bound, and carried them about everywhere in all sorts of languages. So you see that while men have had much to do with the Bible, what is in the Bible came truly from God. It is just as if he had spoken all of it with his own voice. It is just as if he had written all of it with his own hand. It is just as if some day the nations had seen a brightness in the sky coming nearer and nearer. At last they saw it was a glorious hand holding a book, and when it was come nigh and some man bolder than the rest ventured to put out his hand and take it from the air where it sparkled and flashed, he found it to be the Bible. Would he not call it God's Book? Would he not say that God made it and brought it to us? Most certainly. And yet the book would not be more heavenly and divine than it now is.

God made the Bible, and it is the *only* book he ever made. Some other books *pretend* to be his, but it is only a pretense. You would only have to read them a little to see plainly that they never could have come from such a being as God, they have so many foolish, untrue, and bad things in them. So the Bible stands alone. It is an only child. It has no brother or sister among books. God has never given any other volume. He never will give any other, though the world should last a million of years. However large our libraries may get to be, and however beautiful and costly and famous some of the books that will be found in them, not one of them will deserve to be called divine—unless the Bible be among them. If this *be* among them, though but an old and rude and battered copy, it is worth vastly more than all the rest of the volumes on those long and loaded shelves. They are the works of men—of the men we call Plato, Cicero, Locke, Milton, and so on—but this is the only book in the wide world of which God is the author.

There is but one divine book, but this one contains a great deal. It has histories, biographies, poems, proverbs, parables, letters, philosophies, prophecies. As you have already been told, it contains the laws of God's empire, with many helps toward understanding and using them. Besides these, it has what is called the Gospel—

an account of the way in which people who have broken these laws may be forgiven and made better, and at last brought to heaven. That we may better understand and use the Law and Gospel many narratives are given us. We are told of the creation of the world, of our first parents and how they fell into sin, and of many early ages of which we have no other history. We are made to see how patriarchs, saints, kings, and nations lived, age after age—how God dealt with them—and so are made to see what sort of beings men are, what God is, and how he governs the world. Sometimes he sends angels down, sometimes he teaches and warns men in dreams, sometimes prophets and holy men are made to do great wonders in his name, that the good may be helped and the bad punished, and all men know that there is a God to be feared—and to be loved also, for see what a melting story is told in the New Testament of how God so loved us as to give his Son to die for us. What a holy life that Saviour lived, what wise and helpful words he spoke, what wonderful things he did, how sadly he was treated, and how cruelly at last men nailed him to a cross and left him there in agony and blood till he was dead —all that sinners might be saved from sin and ruin! Then follows the story of those who loved him and undertook to tell the world about him, and to persuade men to love and serve him—what they suffered, what they did, what they said, and what success they had and will have in the world—all told in many chapters and books. Scattered largely through and among these books is knowledge for the ignorant, strength for the weak, succor for the tempted, songs for the devout, maxims for living, consolations for dying, truth and holy motives, and " powers of the world to come " for all men.

There is in Paris a famous museum and picture gallery. They call it the Louvre. There one sees, among other valuable things and old things, what is by far the oldest of all. What is it? You would, perhaps, think it a painted stick with something of ornament about it, but you would be told that it is the gold scepter of Charlemagne, one of the most ancient of French monarchs. It is about a thousand years old. You would have to go back through fathers and grandfathers some thirty lives before you would come to the time when that scepter was new. You think of all that has happened in that long time, and which that golden rod could have seen had it been a living thing, and you almost look on it with awe, it is so old. Yes, but you know of another scepter older still. It is not made of gold and jewels—it is not in the shape of a knotty rod—it is in the form of a *book*, but not less a scepter for that, for it means just what scepter means, namely, royal government, the Government of God. The Bible is the oldest scepter in the world, the oldest of sceptered books.

I have among my books some that are very old, and that have long been ruling the world like kings. They were written hundreds, and a few of them thousands, of years ago. But by far the oldest book I have is the Bible. On opening it at the title-page you might find that it was printed only ten years since, and the cover is fresh and the leaves are still delicately white, but for all that it is not only the oldest book I have, but the oldest anybody has. I mean that its thoughts were written out a long, long time ago, and that the earliest of them were written long before those of any other book in the world. It is the patriarch of books. It goes back to the time when mankind itself was hardly more than a little child. Since it was written walls and towers of solid rock have given way, cities have risen and prospered and perished. Empires have been set up, made famous, had long histories, and passed completely away. Generation after generation, wave upon wave, has beat and broken on the shore. But the Bible, that began before them all, has outlived them all. What a Methusaleh! It is antiquity itself. The man who goes about searching for old and venerable things, relics of distant times, things that were old when America and even Europe were young, has not far to go for his best treasure. Let him lay hold of the first Bible that comes to hand.

There was a time when there was only one copy of the Bible; but it was too important a book to remain but one, so men took to copying it off painfully by hand-writing, and often the pages were most beautifully written and pictured by their industrious pens. So Bibles became many. Still they were not many enough for the many people in many lands, and often a Bible was chained in a church or some other public place, so that persons who had none of their own might go there and read it or hear it read. But after a long while men found out how to print with

types, and then Bibles became less costly
and very numerous; and now there is no
book in the world which is so largely
scattered every-where. Millions on millions are printed every year. It has been
printed in more than a hundred languages.
No country of any size where it is not
found. In such countries as ours no book
is so common—almost every person has
one or more copies. Taking the world
through, there is no other book, however
much liked, that has a tenth part of its
readers. Gather the copies together from
every land and they would make mountains and load fleets. It is in the libraries
of scholars, the parlors of the rich, and the
kitchens of the poor. It has become so
cheap that the poorest can buy it : if one
will not buy it he can have it for nothing,
for *nothing* and welcome. If he will not
even take it as a gift in the book form he
must still have it in *some* form. The
words, written or spoken, fill all the air.
They are flying about in all directions like

so many pictured birds, their throats filled with song. Spoken by ministers, taught in Sunday-schools, quoted in books and newspapers, sworn by the profane, praised by friends, abused by enemies—its sacred truths enter every man whether he will or not. The doors and windows of his soul cannot be shut close enough to shut them out. At eye and ear they lie in wait from morning to night, and almost from night to morning, to find some chance for entering. They are already within, and are hiding in every corner of the memory, waiting with keen eyes for a fit time to rush forth and occupy all the chambers of the soul. It is well. God's Book needs to come down among men as come the star-showers in November; nay, as come the showers of rain which manage to touch every blade of grass and wash every tree-leaf in the whole country—thickly, thickly. Every human being surely needs a copy of the Bible which he can read and study by himself, far more than the night needs

stars or the dry earth needs rain, and good
men mean that the time shall come when
every one shall have it. But even now
the Bible is the most widely circulated of
all books.

And it is the truest of books. It is
perfectly true from beginning to end, not
a single falsehood or mistake in all its
thousand pages—a thing that cannot be
said of any other book that ever was
written. I once thought, as perhaps some
of you may now think, that what is
printed must of course be true, but that,
I assure you, was a very considerable time
ago. I soon learned that the very wisest
and best book that man ever made has a
great many false things in it, meant or
not meant, and that some books are false
almost from beginning to end. Now the
Bible is very different from any of these,
as you would suppose from the fact that
God is the author of it. As it came from
his hands there was not the smallest untrue thing in it, from the first page to the

last. God has made no mistake in any of his writings, and far be it from us to think that he means to deceive anybody. He is too wise to do the one thing, and too good to do the other. The Bible is like a clear, still spring of water. If you look into it you see yourselves, the overhanging branch, and the blue sky, just as they really are. So by looking into the Bible we see every thing just as it is. There is no crack in the looking-glass: the pictures in it look precisely like the things they stand for. So you must not fail to believe every thing the true Bible says. Whoever dares to say, " It is not so," does not mind what he says—God's Book is right and true against all the world. It is safe to venture our lives, and even our *souls*, on what it says. I would not care to venture such things on even some mathematical books I have seen. But the Bible is a great deal truer than any science or mathematics that ever men put together.

Another and still better thing which I

wish to tell you about the Bible is, that it is the purest and holiest of books. True books may be bad. ˙ Some real things are just as vile and corrupting as they can be. Satan himself is a fact, and what a dreadful and wicked fact he is ! So I want to tell you that, in addition to all in the Bible being true, all in it is pure and holy. Not the least evil thing in it. It gives no bad advice, no bad laws. It encourages no wrong feelings nor thoughts, but, on the contrary, discourages them. The histories it tells, the songs it sings, the letters it sends to us, are such that the more we read them the better we are likely to be.

The whitest leaf of your newest book is not so clear and white as are all the truths this holy Book teaches. We call it the *Holy* Scriptures, and it is a true name. If we should do just as it tells us, our hearts and lives would be as clean and white as the newest snow. Of course I do not deny that there are other books in the world that deserve to be called good, very good, too; but not one of them is good like the Bible. Do you suppose there is any book besides this that has not some spot of sin about it? I tell you, No! No sinning man ever made a sinless book. No muddy spring ever sent out water clear as crystal. There is always something evil in the book to show what sort of a person it came from. And often the book is so bad that one does not want even to touch it with his finger. We look at it with loathing. We put it into the fire with the tongs. Nothing short of fire will clean and sweeten it. It does us good to see it vanish in flame and smoke. Lately, tons of such books have been destroyed in our cities by the magistrates, and tons more remain to be destroyed. Heap up the fuel, kindle it in a hundred places at once, loud let the fires roar— they never had a better work to do, these books are so unclean. But that Book that comes from God is like God—purest and holiest of books, as God is the purest and holiest of beings.

Some of you may wonder to hear a book called strong and mighty. You have heard of mighty men, and the mighty ocean, and a mighty wind; but then these things are either very large things or they can *do* wonderful things. The Bible is not large; even a little child can carry it about. It has no strong arms with which to lift and to smite. No, but for all that the Bible is mighty. It can do great and wonderful things. It has done them. It has made proud men humble. It has made angry men calm and gentle. Swearing men, stealing men, lying men, selfish men, hating and murdering men, it has made over into quite new persons, teaching them to dread and hate their old sins as so much new poison. Untold times it has done that hardest of all things, making the wicked good. In this way it has before now defeated armies, made and unmade empires, saved nations from ruin,

and made them good, happy, and great.
This is great doing. It is what no other
book ever did or can do. No other book
ever changed men's characters, and made
wicked hearts holy, and washed vile lives
clean. You can wash clean the outside of
cups and platters—when our garments get
black with wearing, much soap and much
rubbing will make them white again.
But such things as wicked hearts and lives
defy all human washing. God has to step
in with his great power. And this power
he has hid in his own book. Here is
water and soap and fire for the unclean
souls of men. It never gets soiled itself
in cleansing others. Have you never
heard that it is " the power of God unto
salvation?" Of course it is mightier
than even the power of Satan—which
some books are. They are so vile and
mischievous, it seems as if Satan were in
them. And he is. They are Satan in the
book form. But the Bible is mightier
than they, as God's power is mightier

than Satan's. So the Bible will at last overcome all the books written against it, just as a great warrior, after standing up calmly for awhile amid the strokes and thrusts of his puny enemies, as if to allow them to do their worst, at last lifts himself to his full stature, and whirls among their ranks his glittering sword, and at once wins the field without a dent in his armor or loss of a feather from his plume —so will the Bible prove itself the mightiest of books.

It is the most useful of books. Is the light useful, without which we cannot see or be warm or be healthy? Is the air useful, without which we cannot breathe? Is it useful to be true and pure and kind and just and unselfish and loving and generous and noble and good? Is it useful to be everlastingly saved and happy in heaven? Then is the Bible useful—the most useful book the world has ev known—for it does more to make what they should be than any an other books. Put all others in one scale and the Bible in the other, the Bible would weigh them all down. I mean that the Bible is *worth* more to the world than all other books put together, however good and famous they may be. The world could get along better without them than without it. Men could not get along without the Bible at all. By it they learn the will of God. By it they are mightily persuaded to do that will. It shows them heaven, and how to gain it—hell, and how to shun it. It holds men back from folly and crime, and pushes them toward wisdom and goodness as with the hand of a giant. It shows men how to live and how to die. No such comforter as the Bible! When afflicted people can find no comfort and strength anywhere else they can find it here. Death itself can be made to smile and seem the best of friends by listing to its courageous words. It has n the world the best knowledge, the homes, the best society, the best gov-

ernments, the best characters and hopes
and prospects it has. Take away it and
that Holy Spirit who goes with it, and the
earth would soon become too bad and
miserable to be lived in. It stands up for
all true and right things like a mighty
champion, and if people would only let it
have its way it would soon make these
earthly deserts almost as delightful as
heaven. This is what we are expecting it
will do. This is what it is aiming to do.
And by and by it will succeed gloriously.
We do not know exactly *when*, but that
the time will come, sooner or later, is a
sure matter. Some think they see signs
of its coming even now. Just as a certain
look of the sky shows that the fruitful
shower is at hand—just as the ruddy
streak gives token of the near day—so
what the Bible is now doing more and
more every year to bless and save men
gives sign of a great future. And when
that great future is come, and all the earth
is swimming in the golden light which the

Bible has poured, no one will dare to ask or answer such an absurd question as, " Is the Bible the most useful of books?" Yesterday the name of the Bible was Struggle, to-day it is Success, to-morrow it will be Triumph. And if all the good it has done, is doing, and will do could be brought together, it would make mountains greater than the Alps, landscapes fairer than Moses saw from Pisgah, skies brighter than bend over Chaldean shepherds. The Bible is worth its weight, we will not say in gold, but in *souls*.

Looking back, we find no book so old as the Bible; looking forward, we find none so sure never to perish or get out of date. It has already outlasted generations and empires—it is sure to outlast all generations and empires yet to come. Of no other book can this be said. When you hear some other book, say the poems of Milton, called *immortal*, and the newspapers saying over and over that it will never die, you may venture to say that it is by no means sure to live a hundred years more. Good books and great books have been lost before now. Nothing but their names have come down to us—sometimes not even so much. The last copy was burned in some great fire. Wars and troublous times came and swept them into dark corners and closets, never to be found more. What has happened may happen again. I should be afraid to say of any book you could bring me, save one, however famous it may now be and however many copies of it may be scattered through the world, that it will last a thousand years. It may not last ten. But there is one book that will never get trampled to pieces under the hoofs of stormy times— one book which no neglect nor violence nor craft will be able to put an end to. It has been tried. Many Bibles have been set a burning. Many have been buried in dungeons and dead languages, and bidden to lie there and never rise more. The book has had many enemies, and they have done their best to kill it with jesting and scoffing and arguing and persecuting. But it could not be killed. It has shown no faculty for dying. It never had more breath in it than it has to-day. Never was it so famous and, on the whole, so powerful. It is quite safe to say that neither the Bible nor any part will ever perish. Single copies of it may be destroyed—people may tear up or burn up the covers, the leaves, so that not a single printed word of it shall remain. What is to hinder? The Bible will burn like other books. Of course paper will kindle, and flame, and turn to smoke and ashes. But other copies will be left. Faithful souls here and there will keep the seed safe all over the world. God will always have an ark to carry it safely through every deluge. It will last as long as the world does. It was made to last *forever*, and it will. It has an iron constitution. And when the last day comes, and the world is set ablaze, and the trees and houses and books, and even rocks and waters, catch like tinder, and good men go up in fiery chariots to heaven, then the Bible unhurt will go up with it and be studied and honored forever. Immortal Book, undying as the men it enlightens and saves!

Most books soon cease to be useful if they do not cease to exist. Circumstances alter. The times get beyond them. Once they answered a purpose, but now they are good for nothing. When a book becomes good for nothing it ought to be called *dead*, and dead most books become very soon after they are printed. Nothing more can be got out of them. If a man reads them the second time he loses his time. They will count in a catalogue, and, with a fair binding, will make a fair show on the shelves of a library—that is all. But the Bible is not like such books. It never gets out of date. It suits one time as well as another. The more one reads it the more he finds in it. It is like those gold mines which grow richer the deeper one digs. Lasting, *inexhaustible* mines we call them. Instead of becoming waste places, silent, deserted, littered with the broken tools and wastage of other days, the roar of cheerful labor deepens around them from age to age.

In short, the Bible is a *perfect* book. No fault can reasonably be found with it. It is just what the world needs to have in a book from God. It has the best possible object in view, and it is as well suited to gain its object as book can possibly be. Were one to add any thing to it he would harm it—were one to take away any thing from it he would harm it. So if one should make this and that chapter, this and that verse, change places. Hence we are threatened with a great punishment if we try to alter the book in any way whatever. It is because the Bible is just right as it is. Of course it must be, coming as it does from God. Other books come from imperfect men, and it would be foolish to expect a single one of them to be without fault. But this book comes from a perfect Being, and it would be equally foolish to expect in it any fault whatever. It has none—no scar, no wrinkle, no such thing. Just the book to come down from heaven —just the book for God to give. Of what other book can as much be said? I never saw any, never expect to see any. I have passed through many great libraries. Hundreds of thousands of volumes stood on the right hand and on the left, many of them in costly bindings and famous the world over, but I knew that not one of them was a perfect book. That glorious poem—every body knows it has its blemishes. The same of that best book of travels, of that best book of fiction, of that best book of science. We have but to look sharply, and lo! something that might be bettered. Lo! things here that should be added and things there that should be subtracted. Really, it is only a piece of a book. Really, it is a body without a hand or a foot, perhaps even

without a head. It was to have been expected. A man who thinks that such mis-
taken and sinful half-beings as men can
make any other than half-books is very poor
at thinking. But the Bible is no cripple,
no sick man. No miracle need be wrought
on it to give it perfect soundness. The
rose joins with the lily in its cheek. Every
rounded limb is there in just the right
proportion. There is no weakness in its
strength, no slowness in its swiftness, no
homeliness in its beauty, no sickness in
its health. In short, it is a *perfect* book.

We love persons—O, how dearly sometimes! Your fathers and mothers love
you so much that they could die for you.
Almost any of them would do for you as
did the freezing mother for her infant—
taking the shawl from her own shoulders
and wrapping it round the child that it
might be found in the morning warm and
living, and herself cold, stiff, dead. After
this manner *your* mothers love you, and it
is to be hoped that you know what it is

to love them back again. Something of the same tenderness is often felt toward things that are not persons; for example, toward pictures of dead or absent friends, or books which they have left as keepsakes. Some people love some books almost as dearly as if the lifeless things had hearts with which to give love in return, especially people who make it their business to read and study. Such often get so strongly attached to the favorite histories, or poems, or books of science—perhaps to the best books of all these sorts—that it is hard to be away from them for a single day. But let me tell you that no book has ever been loved like the Bible—not by all people. Some have even hated it, and would have been glad to burn up every copy of it in the world. But greatly loved is it by good people of the best sort. Some have loved it so much that they would rather part with any thing else than with it. They have tenderly pressed it to their lips and bosoms in feeble token of how precious their hearts felt it to be. Rather than give it up they have given up all other property, and even life itself—dying by prisons, by fire, and by sword. " Bring me the Book," said a dying man who had written many famous books himself. " What book ? " said his son. " There is but one Book," was the feeble answer. It was the *Bible* that dying man wanted. No other book did he care for then. What Sir Walter Scott felt just as he was leaving the world others have felt for many long years—especially in sorrowful times. Then the good man looks toward the Bible with something of the .feeling he has toward heaven. Somehow it has a faculty for drawing hearts to itself—like that sometimes possessed by a most lovely and amiable living person whose voice is sweetness itself, whose eyes are like the dove's, and whose tender, pure, generous, winsome soul shines out of winsome form and feature as the thousand lights of the evening worship stream through the painted windows of a cathedral.

My young friends, I want to have this sacred and glorious Book dear to *you.* It ought to be. You have no better friend. It has been the friend of your fathers and mothers, never so far back. It has been the friend of your country from the beginning, and without it you would never have had a country worth having. When your forefathers came across the Atlantic to build new homes in what was then but wild woods they felt that the most precious thing they brought with them was a book —*this* Book. They came because of it— came that they might obey it as they understood it, and make a new nation in which the Bible should be more than king and Elizabeth less than queen. Some held it bound in satin and gold, some in dress as coarse and cheap as the printer and binder could well give it, but to all it was the Book of books. They taught it to their children more carefully than they did

any thing else. They meant that those
who came after them should love and live
by the Bible even as they themselves did.
It would have pained them much to think
the time would ever come when the dear
country in the making of which they suffered so much would think little of what
was so precious to them. I hope that
time never *will* come. Good men mean,
if possible, to prevent its coming. This
is, partly, why we have Sunday-schools.
This is why catechisms and hymns and
Bible verses are taught you. This is why
so many little books and papers are printed
for you by many Christian publishers, and
why some ministers get together the parish children by themselves and preach to
them, as I am now doing to you. It is to
bring those who in a few years will be
the men and women of the land to love and
live by the Bible. And if we succeed it will
be a happy thing for the land which our
fathers so loved and prayed for, and, some
of them, died for; for the Bible is like a

certain man whom they called a landscape-gardener. He made it his business to take a rude spot of country, sometimes a few acres and sometimes thousands of acres, and so change it as to make it most delightful. He cut away at one point, he planted at another; he carried away stones, he covered great rocks with green creepers, he drained swamps and made barren places rich, he made lakes and streams and fountains, he opened stretches of fine prospects, he laid out drives and walks that wound in and out to pleasant points of view and cosy nooks and grand outlooks. So the country became at last a picture. It was a wilderness; now it is a garden, and people come great distances to see it. Pleasure-seekers wander about it in gay groups, the sickly are wheeled carefully through its pleasant shades and sunshines, painters paint it, poets sing it, all eyes feast on its beauties. All are refreshed, all are delighted, all praise it and the man whose taste and skill made it what it is.

"Who could have thought it! What a wonderful change from the poor, common, forbidding spot this was once to what it is now! One who could make so much out of so little—roses out of weeds, fountains out of sands, and a delightful garden out of a tiresome spot—is a great genius, and deserves to be famous." And famous he becomes. He is sent for from near and far. Other waste places wish to be built up after the same beautiful manner. The demand for him is pressing. Applications for his services stream in day and night. He can set his own prices. His fortune is made.

See what the Bible is. See what it will do for our place and country and world if we succeed in getting the children to treat it as it ought to be treated—if we get them to honor it and submit themselves to it as that spot of rough land I have just spoken of was submitted to the landscape-gardener. It will be quite a different parish, quite a different country, quite

a different world. It will be as if the
wand of a mighty magician had been
stretched over it. There will be fountains
in the wilderness and streams in the desert.
Unsightly things will disappear. Their
places will be filled with all that is rich
and fair—with truth and good will, and
education and industry, and temperance
and honesty, and good order and godliness,
and all the virtues. Want will be cured
as by famous medicine. Hurts by sin and
sorrow will be tenderly bound up by numberless good Samaritans on numberless
roads to Jericho. In short, the change
will be wondrously great in homes, schools,
parishes, society, governments.

I do not know how many fine landscapes
you have seen, but this I know, that you
never yet saw any half as fair as the Bible
can make . out of any place, however
dreary, that is once fairly put into its
hands. What a name such a great artist
should have! What a loud call there
should be for him! As people send for

that famous landscape-gardener from every quarter, and will do almost any thing to secure his help, so should we be most anxious to have that greater landscape-gardener, the Bible, set fairly to work on all this wicked and sorrowful world. Nothing else will so freshen and brighten it. Nothing else will do it any lasting good. Its chapters and verses are what the lamps are to the dark city streets, what the stars are to the lone, dark roads of the country. Men get lost and perish without them.

Such a book as this—so true, so instructive, so pure, so useful, so mighty for good, so divine, indeed, the only divine book in all the world—you ought to make much of. Read it much. Try to understand it. Hang up hundreds of its verses in rich frames in your memories. Believe all it tells you, do all it bids you, get others to do the same. Then you will grow up to be such men and women as God loves, and the world needs, and heaven will be sure to get at last.

Heaven ! I see its gates open—its gates of pearl. I see many going in, some of you among them. Every one of them presses a Book to his bosom. "Ho, far away traveler, what is it thou dost clasp so tightly and fondly, even though thine eyes are just filling with the strange glories of the city whose builder is God?" No answer. He is too full of the wonders he sees and hears to heed my voice though it sweep toward and by him like the prayer of the publican or of an apostle. But God heeds, and a softly flying thought comes to me from him, saying, That book is the Bible. It has cheered him and guided him; it has been light and food and shelter and rest and sword to him. To it he owes what he is, and where he is. He has carried that book on his heart all through the rough journey, and, now that he has come to the end, no wonder that his fingers, which just begin to glow in the golden light of heaven, close on it more fondly than ever. No wonder!

> "May this blest volume ever lie
> Close to *my* heart and near my eye,
> Till life's last hour my soul engage,
> And be my chosen heritage."

THE END.

www.ingramcontent.com/pod-product-compliance
Lightning Source LLC
Chambersburg PA
CBHW021112020726
47500CB00003B/718